A VISION A DAY KEEPS THE KILLER AWAY

PIPER ASHWELL PSYCHIC P.I., BOOK 1

KELLY HASHWAY

To Ayla with love

CHAPTER ONE

"Got another one for you, sweetheart." Detective Thomas Ashwell—or as I call him, "Dad"—slaps a manila folder down on my desk and takes the seat opposite me. He never announces himself or knocks before entering my small office in the strip mall on Fifth Street.

I meet Dad's blue-green eyes briefly before placing my half-empty coffee cup from Marcia's Nook down next to my laptop and reaching for the folder. Flipping it open, I scan the pages inside, not taking in anything more than a name: Veronica Castell. I quickly shut the folder and shove it across the desk. "Give me something I can use, Dad. There's nothing here but a police report. Even the common public knows I need a personal effect if you want my help."

My father drums his fingers together, his lips pursed as he studies me. He knows I'm going to take the case. Yet we do this song and dance every time he walks into my office. "Remember the Belinda Maxwell case?"

I pick up my pen and click it incessantly. "How could I forget? I wouldn't be sitting here today if I hadn't gotten involved in that case." Belinda Maxwell was a beloved child actress, so when she was abducted by the most vile and psychotic man, Heathrow Livingstone, the entire country searched high and low for her. Every news station flashed Belinda's picture on the screen, a six-year-old image of loveliness. Belinda's aunt happened to live two blocks from my parents at the time, and she walked door to door with Belinda's picture and a locket Belinda usually wore.

Dad rubs his gray goatee, his eyes peering into mine. "You never told me what made you ask to hold Belinda's locket when her aunt showed up at our house."

"Just a feeling I had." I'd had "feelings" my whole life, but I'd ignored them. My extrasensory abilities decided to tune in the moment I saw the locket, and I knew I had to touch it. By the looks of it, the locket had been torn off Belinda's neck, most likely when she'd been taken. It was when I asked to hold the locket that I got my first vision. I didn't see Belinda. Instead, I saw a fleeting glimpse of Heathrow Livingstone, Belinda's abductor.

"You didn't tell me about your vision until later that night."

I didn't want to tell anyone what I saw. I was completely freaked out. Not only because I was seeing things but because Livingstone was downright scary with his crazy brown and gray hair that looked like he'd stuck his fingers in an electrical outlet and his steely gray eyes. "I thought I was losing my mind at twelve years old." Of course, I later learned that what I did—and still do—is called psychometry. I read the energy off objects.

Dad's brow furrows, and he sets his jaw in his look of disapproval. "I never thought you were crazy, Piper."

Mom had been terrified for me, but Dad had seen psychics do what I did, so he handled everything calmly. "No, you didn't. You asked Belinda's aunt to come back with the locket." The visions only got stronger and more frequent as I held the locket tightly in my fist. I heard Livingstone's low, sinister voice as he threatened to cut off all Belinda's hair and send it to her parents in a plastic bag with a ransom note demanding twenty million dollars. I found her one week later. Heathrow threw himself off the Weltunkin Bridge that night. The police dragged his corpse out of the river hours later. It was weeks of news crews interviewing me after that.

If my father hadn't been a highly regarded police detective, I probably would have been seen as a kid who had tried to prank the nation and got lucky. Instead, I became the police force's go-to for missing persons cases.

Sixteen years later, I'm a twenty-eight-year-old private investigator, specializing in missing persons cases, though my visions aren't limited to those alone. I've found a few missing dogs and located a murder weapon a convenient store robber tried to bury after fleeing the scene. I've come to accept this is my life because my abilities don't really give me any other choice.

"Lost in thought?" Dad leans forward, picking up the folder and opening it to the pages I didn't bother to read. "Veronica Castell is the daughter of a very wealthy business man, Victor Castell. He likes to stay under the radar, a silent partner almost. At least that's what he had hoped. Turns out plenty of people know about his billions. He's sure his daughter's disappearance is the result of a kidnapping and that a ransom note will turn up soon enough."

"Let me guess. Mr. Castell wants me to step in, have some visions, and find Veronica before he has to dish over a few million in exchange for his daughter's life." I polish off the rest of my toasted almond coffee. "Why is it that no one seems to understand how psychometry works? I only see glimpses—whispers. I can't rush what I do."

Dad smiles. "Whispers. You're still calling them that?"

I toss the empty cup in the trash can next to my desk and sit up straight in my chair. "What can I say? I was a genius at twelve."

"Chip off the old block." Dad stands and motions to the coffee cup in the garbage can. "Can I buy you another? I have a few minutes before I have to be back at the station."

"No thanks. I want to go over the file and set up a meeting with Mr. and Mrs. Castell. Does this afternoon work for you?"

Dad huffs. "You can't always be the job, Piper. Learn to take breaks. When was the last time you had coffee with a friend?"

A friend. The concept is almost foreign to me. Though I do sort of consider Marcia Woodell my friend. I see her every morning when I go to Marcia's Nook for my coffee and elephant ear. And of course I browse the books as well. Speaking of, I finished my book last night. "I'm planning to see Marcia in a bit, maybe for lunch." It's a partial truth. I probably will go on my lunch hour.

Dad nods but doesn't look convinced. "Call me when you've made arrangements to see the Castells, and I'll pick you up." He starts for the door but hesitates before opening it. "Oh"—he says with his back to me—"Detective Brennan will be coming with us. He's officially been promoted to my partner."

"Well, isn't that just...?" Words elude me, so I settle for shaking my head even though Dad can't see it. Mitchell Brennan isn't the easiest person to get along with. He thinks he's God's gift to women. And while he's attractive with his green eyes, dark hair, and six foot toned frame, he has a lot of growing up to do for a thirty-year-old man.

The soft click of the door as it shuts notifies me Dad's left, so I scan the police report. These things don't help me at all, and quite frankly, I hate reading them. I like to go into my investigations knowing as little as possible. That might sound backward, but my whispers are what help me find a person. Evidence can be misleading. My abilities, while cloudy puzzle pieces at best, are what I rely on. I locate the contact number and address for Victor Castell. I punch the number into my phone and bring it to my ear.

On the third ring, a gruff voice answers. "Victor Castell."

"Mr. Castell, this is Piper Ashwell."

"Who?"

I roll my eyes and rub the tension building across my forehead. "Piper Ashwell. I'm working with Detective Thomas Ashwell on your daughter's case."

"Oh, I didn't realize. I'm sorry, Detective, but I've been dealing with reporters all morning."

"I'm a private investigator, actually." Dad owes me big time for not talking to Victor Castell about bringing me on to the case. Most people think I'm a fraud, Belinda Maxwell's case long forgotten after all these years.

"I see. I hadn't realized the police were bringing in a PI to help locate my daughter."

"I'm Detective Ashwell's daughter." I speak slowly, knowing the man is distraught. "I often help with missing persons cases. I have a special...talent for it."

"Well then, I suppose I should thank you."

"No need. I would like to come talk to you and your wife, though. I was hoping I could stop by this afternoon if that works for you." I swivel in my chair, staring out at the dreary fall day. I usually love fall and all its bright colors, but today looks more like winter. Gray.

"Of course. I've canceled all my meetings today." His voice cracks, and he tries to cover it up with a cough. My heart breaks for him. He must be worried sick about his daughter. "Does three o'clock work for you?"

"Absolutely. I'll see you then." Before I end the call, I can't help adding, "We'll find your daughter, Mr. Castell. You can count on it." I slip my phone into the back pocket of my black slacks, cursing myself for making an empty promise. So far, I've solved every missing persons case I've worked on, but I haven't always solved them on time. I remember the names of the people I was too late to save—the people I brought home to be buried by loved ones.

I reach for my coffee, my fingers finding nothing since I already finished it. I guess I'll be going to see Marcia after all.

CHAPTER TWO

Marcia's Nook is exactly twenty-three steps from my office. We share the strip mall, though my section of it is much smaller, occupying one single office. Marcia's Nook takes up the rest of the space. It's really the perfect setup. I love caffeine, books, and baked goods. Plus, I hate to stop working to eat, so I usually wander here, grab some food, and take it back to my desk. Dad calls me a loner, but really I just like the quiet.

The bell over the door dings as I enter. Marcia is usually busy making sure all the displays, both for books and food, are perfectly designed, but today she's nowhere in sight as I look around. The café is to my right, the wall butting up against my office, and to the left, the books are arranged on shelves of different sizes. I head left, intent on finding a new book to read tonight. I pass the children's books with the beanbag chairs set up in the corner for the weekly lap sit. Marcia is probably the sweetest woman I've ever met. Not only does she run this place, but she insists on free programs for kids and adults. She often has authors come in for readings or writing workshops, and the children's programs range from lap sit to book signings to character days where she hires actors in costumes fashioned after whatever book character is popular at the time.

Following the side wall to the back, I stop in the mystery section. I scan the shelves, but I've read just about everything. One perk to living by myself and rarely ever dating is I can breeze through a book every few nights, averaging two to three a week depending on length. I pick up a book with a familiar sounding title, but I can't quite place the story. I flip it over to read the back when I hear footsteps on the laminate wood flooring.

"Piper, back so soon?"

I turn to see Marcia, still wearing her apron, which looks like it's splattered with a reddish brown spice. My extra sensitive sense of smell immediately picks up on the cinnamon. "Today requires extra caffeine and a good book." I raise the book in my hand so she can see the cover. "I just can't remember if I've read this one."

Marcia squints her hazel eyes at me. With her espresso hair and red highlights, petite five-one frame, and pale skin with freckles dotting her nose and cheekbones, she's nothing short of adorable. I see the way men look at her when they enter the store. Add her curves to the rest of the package and she gets offers for dates on a daily basis.

"Piper?" Marcia says. "Did you hear me?"

I shake my head. "Sorry. I guess I zoned out again."

"That's a used book." She gestures to my hand. "Remember? It was yours. You brought it to me in exchange for store credit."

I eye the cover again, allowing my mind to center on the book. An image of a slightly younger Marcia settling into the leased space fills my head. *My twenty-five-year-old self jumps on her offer to exchange a bunch of books I'd already read for store credit.* "Thanks," I say. "I just moved into a new place, and I don't exactly have much spare cash at the moment."

"You were reading your own history off that book, weren't you?" Marcia lowers her voice even though we're the only two people in the store. She knows I don't like to draw attention to myself when my abilities take over in public. And I especially hate when they make me speak out loud like I just did.

"Like I said, it's been that kind of day."

"I'm not sure how the book got on that shelf to begin with. I guess a customer put it back there by mistake." She reaches for it, and I place the book in her hand.

I avoid the used books to keep things like this from happening. I motion toward the café. "I could use another toasted almond coffee. Large," I add, rubbing my temples.

"I have aspirin in my purse if you need some," Marcia says, her voice soft and full of concern.

I never take aspirin when I'm working a case. I find it messes with my abilities. "No, it's fine. The coffee should do the trick." That and the nap I plan to take after I drink it. If I don't rest up before a case, I feel drained after my visions.

Marcia walks around the bakery counter to get my coffee. "Have you eaten anything since the elephant ear you had this morning?"

"No, but it's only been..." I look up at the clock on the wall, which is made with books that have numbers in the titles. Marcia got the idea from a meme going around on Facebook a few years back and said she had to replicate it. Right now, the hour hand is pointing to *Murder at Midnight* and the minute hand is pointing to *Three Times the Trouble*.

Marcia follows my gaze. "A quarter after twelve."

"How did that happen?" I rub my forehead.

"You know what they say about manic Mondays. This place was packed all morning. This is the first lull I've had." Marcia caps my to-go cup and puts it on the counter. "Now, what can I get you to eat? I just made apple turnovers."

She knows I don't join most of the country's fascination with all things pumpkin at this time of year. "That sounds perfect."

She shakes her head at me. "I swear, if I ate the way you do, I wouldn't fit through the door in the mornings." She laughs as she places an apple turnover in a bag for me.

"Trust me, you'd hate having my metabolism. I can't gain weight if I tried. I wish I had your curves." Back in high school, when my junior year English teacher assigned "gaunt" as one of our vocabulary words, a girl in the back of the class, Laura Flemming, announced, "Thin and bony, just like Piper." That word has haunted me ever since.

"Every woman wants what God didn't give her, right?" She rings me up, and I use my phone to pay. I never have any cash on me. Ever. I'm a prime target for identity theft because I do absolutely everything online. Of course, I doubt anyone would try to steal my identity, assuming I'd use my psychic abilities to track them down and put them in a jail cell.

"As usual, thanks for keeping me well fed and caffeinated." I hold up my coffee and pastry bag. I start for the door when I remember I didn't find a book. "Oh." I whirl around, and Marcia waves me into the back storage room.

"Come on. I didn't get to unpack the newest arrivals yet." She holds the door open for me.

"You are the absolute best." Sometimes I suspect Marcia knows I don't have many friends. At least not ones I see or talk to often. She goes out of her way to be nice to me and to indulge my quirks.

"This box over here has some new mysteries in it." She grabs a box cutter and slices the packaging tape down the middle. "I'll be spending my afternoon getting these into the system and shelving them. I have to swap out displays, too."

"Oh, well if you haven't entered them in the system, I can't exactly buy one yet."

She waves the comment away. "It's fine. I'll take a picture of the information I need and enter it later. You won't be able to pay for it today is all."

"Are you sure about this? I don't want you going through all this trouble just for me. I could watch TV tonight like a normal person."

She cocks her head at me. "You are anything but normal, Piper, which is why I adore you." She opens the box and motions for me to start digging through it.

There are two new books I've been waiting for, but I don't dare tell her that. I'll take one now and come back for the other when I pay my bill for this one. I grab the one on top, letting proximity be the deciding factor. "Thank you. I wish I could stay to help you shelve these, but I have an appointment this afternoon for a new case I'm working on."

"Which I'm sure is much more important, so go." She shoos me through the storage room door as I balance the book and bag in one hand and my coffee in the other.

"Thanks again!" I call as I use my back to open the door.

She gives a wave and then disappears into the kitchen.

I awkwardly balance the book between my thumb and forefinger, while holding the bag between my pinky and ring finger, so I can read the back cover copy. I'm so engrossed in the story I don't even see Mitchell Brennan until he grabs me by my forearms to stop me from walking right into him.

"Oh, hi," I say, looking up at him, noticing his hunter

green shirt is making his eyes appear even darker than usual.

"That's much better than being greeted by hot coffee scalding my chest." He lets go of my arms and motions to the cup in my left hand.

"Close call, huh? Glad I didn't singe any chest hair."

He laughs and pats the front of his shirt. "Clean shaven. Not a hair to be found."

"More than I needed to know." I start to walk around him to my office where my "Open" sign still hangs on the door. "Damn, I forgot to flip this thing again."

"I doubt you get many walk-ins," Detective Brennan says, following behind me.

"Can I help you, Detective? I was under the impression you were walking in the other direction." No such luck. I try the door handle but can't manage it with all I'm holding.

"Here. Let me." Detective Brennan steps forward and opens the door for me. "Chivalry isn't completely dead, you know."

I glance up at him since he has a good eight inches on my "five-four on a good day since I never wear heels" stature. "Chivalry, chauvinism, it's all the same in your mind, isn't it?"

"Your words wound me, Piper. Really they do." He places his hand over his heart and smirks.

I roll my eyes since I can't exactly smack the look off his face, considering he's my father's new partner and I'm going to have to work with him whether I hate it or...well, there isn't another alternative.

I walk to my desk, tossing the book and bag down before bringing the coffee to my lips. Not even a large toasted almond is going to help me get through this conversation with Brennan. "You didn't answer my question. Why are you here?"

"Your father sent me."

I cock my head at him. "My father? The one I saw not long ago? The one who told me to call him once I set up a time to meet the Castells? That one?"

Brennan nods, clearly enjoying our banter. At least one of us is.

"Let me guess. You were annoying him so much he decided to send you on an errand just so he didn't have to look at you anymore?" I sit down, taking another slug of coffee before turning to my laptop and pretending I have work to do.

Detective Brennan sits down on the corner of my desk, earning a side-eye from me. "So much hate, Piper. You know what they say. 'The lady doth protest too much.'"

I shut my laptop and stare at him. "Mitchell—"

"Liking the first name basis. Go on." He waves his hand in the air, and I'd love nothing more than to grab it and shove it into my hot coffee.

I take a deep breath, centering myself, which is usually what I do to prepare for a vision, so I'm quite practiced at it. "Let's get something straight. I find you and your superiority complex nothing short of revolting. I tolerate you out of necessity. I accept that I have to work with you, but our relationship—if you can call it that—ends there. Am I making myself clear?"

He stands up and clears his throat. "So what time should I tell your father?"

"Three o'clock. And tell him since he failed to alert Mr. Castell that I'm working the case, I failed to mention he'd be accompanying me this afternoon."

"I guess you failed to mention me as well."

"Actually, I hadn't given you a thought at all." I open my laptop again and click on my email, ignoring Brennan as he walks out of my office.

The truth is, the last thing I want is to have a vision with Mitchell Brennan around. I feel vulnerable when I'm using my abilities, mostly because I never can predict what I'm going to see, hear, feel... I like having Dad around, but Mitchell?

Yes, this is going to be one hell of a case.

CHAPTER THREE

The Castells live in a huge white colonial at the top of Millington Way. I'm not usually impressed with large houses, not wanting to have to clean a space that big, but even I sit up straight in the back seat of Dad's BMW. The house has three balconies on the top floor, which I'm assuming are attached to bedrooms. The ornate black shutters and etched windows look like they belong on a church or castle, not a home in northern Pennsylvania. Though I should be used to it since Weltunkin has become a vacation spot for celebrities looking to escape the hustle and bustle of big cities. If my parents hadn't settled here before Hollywood took over, they never would have been able to afford a place in this town. Hell, I can barely afford my small apartment, but I got a good deal considering my landlord is a friend of Dad's.

"Can you see okay back there?" Detective Brennan asks, lowering his visor so he can see me in the mirror.

I resist the urge to flip him off since Dad is watching me in the rearview mirror. "I can see just fine. In fact, I believe you have a new gray hair on the back of your head." I raise my hand, circling a finger where most men develop a bald spot. "Or maybe that's scalp I'm seeing. It is looking a little thin right around here."

"You two." Dad laughs and shakes his head. "I'm not sure if you hate each other or are secretly harboring feelings of—"

"It's hate," I stop him.

"Ouch, Piper." Brennan flips his visor up and turns to face me as Dad parks. "Hate is a strong word, don't you think?"

"Actually, it's pretty mild, but I'm trying to keep it professional." I unclick my seat belt and open the door. "And speaking of, I'd prefer if you referred to me as Ms. Ashwell. We are on a case." I slam the car door and start for the walkway leading to the front porch. It's lined with lights and some sort of non-flowering plants.

Dad catches up to me, placing his hand on my lower back. "Play nice, please. I have to work with him every day."

"I feel for you," I say, walking up the four steps to the front door.

Dad smirks as he raises his hand to ring the bell.

Footsteps sound, getting louder as they approach the door, which is then slowly opened. The man in front of us is in his late forties, about six-two, with dark hair peppered with gray at his temples. He turns his head to look from Dad to me to Brennan, and I notice his nose comes to a decided point at the end. "Can I help you?"

I flash my PI license, and Dad and Brennan produce their badges. "I'm Piper Ashwell. We spoke on the phone."

"Yes, yes. I'm Victor Castell. I wasn't aware that you were bringing detectives with you, Ms. Ashwell." Castell continues to eye Brennan.

"You already know my father, Detective Thomas Ashwell, and this is his partner, Detective Mitchell Brennan." I gesture briefly behind me but don't allow Brennan to extend his hand. "May we come inside, or do you prefer to talk out here?"

Castell steps aside, his hands gripping the door so tightly his knuckles turn white. "Come in. Please."

I nod as I walk past him into the foyer. A crystal chandelier hangs from the vaulted ceiling, and a large water fountain in the shape of a vase that continually spills water and refills is perched in front of me.

"You have a lovely home," Detective Brennan says, earning him an eye roll from me. Pleasantries are useless at a time like this. The last thing Victor Castell cares about is what we think of his home.

"This way, please." Castell motions to a sitting room to our right. The furnishings are very old-fashioned, making me wonder if the house itself is a family heirloom.

I take a seat on the burgundy couch, which couldn't be harder if it were made out of rock. Dad joins me, while Detective Brennan chooses to stand. Victor Castell sits in an armchair opposite the couch.

"Would any of you care for something to drink? My wife—"

"No, Mr. Castell. We don't want to take up too much of your time. We'll just..." I place my hand on the couch, starting to stand, and my eyes slam shut as my head fills with voices.

"I'll be home again for Thanksgiving. That's really not that far off." Veronica *pulls her legs up under her on the couch.*

"I know, sweetheart. I was just hoping you'd be able to visit a little longer. I took the whole weekend off, thinking we

17

could celebrate my birthday." Victor Castell swirls the brandy in his glass, letting it melt the ice.

"Daddy, there's a huge party this weekend, and I've already promised my friends I'd go. You know how it is." Veronica runs a hand through her wavy brown hair, holding the ends in her fingertips to study them. "Ugh, and I'm in desperate need of a trim. Split ends everywhere."

"I could call Brianna. I'm sure she'd come right over." Castell places his brandy on the coffee table and removes his phone from the back pocket of his gray slacks.

Veronica stands up and walks around the table to her father's side. She reaches up on her toes and kisses his cheek. "Not this time, Daddy. I promise I'll come home for an entire week for Thanksgiving and we can do all the father-daughter things you want."

Victor smiles. "I'll hold you to that promise."

"Piper?" Dad's voice fills my ears as the vision subsides.

I blink a few times, allowing the room to come into focus. "I'm sorry."

Dad studies my face for a moment before turning to Mr. Castell. "Victor, I'm not sure you're aware of my daughter's capabilities."

I hold up my hand to stop him. "Mr. Castell, I understand your daughter was home to celebrate your birthday." I look at him and notice Detective Brennan is standing next to Victor Castell. His eyes staring intently at me. He's never actually witnessed one of my visions. I'm just happy I didn't start screaming or cowering against the couch cushions. As far as visions go, this one was completely mild.

Victor cocks his head at me. "How did you know that?"

Dad clears his throat, but I cut him off before he can explain. "I'm what you'd call a psychic PI. When I'm around objects that hold significance to a missing person, I tend to experience memories of that person."

Victor walks over to the mahogany bar on the opposite side of the room. "I'm sorry, but did you say 'psychic,' as in you *see* things?"

I stifle a sigh. "Yes, sir. I know it's not always easy to believe, but I just witnessed a conversation between you and your daughter. She was sitting on this couch in the very spot I'm occupying now."

"That's a little creepy," Detective Brennan whispers under his breath before turning to see Victor's reaction to my confession.

Dad stands up, directing everyone's attention to him. "Mr. Castell, I can verify that my daughter's abilities are completely real. She has helped the Weltunkin Police Department solve numerous missing persons cases. It's in your best interest to hear her out and answer any questions she may have."

Victor pours himself a brandy and removes the lid from the silver ice bucket.

"Three ice cubes," I say, picturing his glass from my vision. "You drank brandy with exactly three ice cubes, which you swished into the drink to cool it." This time I stand up and move toward him. "You wanted your daughter to stay for the weekend, but she insisted she had already made other plans and would see you for Thanksgiving."

"Did that upset you?" Detective Brennan asks, not concealing the intent behind his question.

I glare at him for a moment before defending Victor. "Mr. Castell, my abilities aren't limited to visions. I could feel how much you love your daughter. I know you had nothing to do with her disappearance." I shoot Brennan another look, which makes him raise his hands in surrender.

"Thank you, Ms. Ashwell." Victor drops three ice cubes into his glass. "Can you tell me what else you saw? Do you know where Veronica is?" His voice is so full of hope. He may not fully believe in my abilities just yet, but he's grasping at any straws I'll give him.

"I'd like to see Veronica's room if you don't mind. That would help." I'm specifically looking for the outfit she was wearing in my vision—black leggings and a long gray sweater that hung off one shoulder. Odds are she wasn't wearing it when she disappeared, though.

"Victor, are you—?" A woman with pin straight, shoulder-length auburn hair walks into the room and stops abruptly when she sees us. "I'm sorry. I didn't realize you had company."

"Darla." Victor reaches out a hand and walks toward the woman. "These are the detectives searching for our daughter."

I can't help wondering if he didn't bother to clarify who I was on purpose.

"Detectives, this is my wife, Darla Castell." Victor takes a large sip of his brandy as Darla nods to each of us.

"Do you have any leads?" she asks, wrapping an arm around her husband's waist.

Dad extends his hand to Mrs. Castell. "I'm Detective Ashwell. My coworkers and I are hoping to find some leads here today."

Mrs. Castell's arm drops to her side, and she steps away from her husband, eyeing him suspiciously. "I don't understand. Why would you find any leads here?"

"No one is accusing anyone, Mrs. Castell," Detective Brennan says, which is rather amusing considering he accused Victor Castell moments earlier.

I step forward, unable to keep up this ridiculous ruse. "Mrs. Castell, I'm afraid I'm the reason everyone is suddenly on edge. I can see from your husband's reaction and choice of words that he doesn't want you to know of my true involvement in this case. You see, I'm a psychic PI, and quite frankly, I'm your best hope for finding your daughter."

Dad smiles at me, but Mrs. Castell's reaction is much the opposite. "A psychic? Is this someone's idea of a joke?" Mrs. Castell looks horrified. "Our daughter is missing. What part of that do you people not understand? To bring a...a..."

Oh lady, you better choose your words carefully.

"A carnival freak show here!" She bursts into tears and rushes from the room before I can go freak show on her ass for that comment.

"I'm so sorry, Ms. Ashwell," Victor says before downing the rest of his brandy. "My wife is beside herself, as I'm sure you can understand."

"Of course," Dad says, knowing I'll have a different reaction if given the opportunity to speak. "Perhaps we could see Veronica's room while you check on your wife, Mr. Castell?"

Victor nods and points toward the hallway. We follow, me shaking my head, Dad squeezing my hand, and Brennan suppressing a smile.

As we walk down the hallway, I take notice of the pictures hanging on the walls. Most are of Veronica through the years. Her dark, wavy hair and pointy nose are very characteristic of her father. Each photograph gives me the vibe of a loving father-daughter relationship. Veronica is definitely a daddy's girl. The question is does she truly love her father or just his money. She wasn't as easy to read in the vision as Victor was. It could be because Veronica's mind was in so many places at once. I saw glimpses of college life—parties, friends, classes. All faint whispers. Nothing concrete. She could have been stressed about an assignment and not sure if going to the party was a good idea, but torn with the idea of disappointing her friends when she was already disappointing her father. I can't know for sure until I see more.

Victor Castell brings us up a staircase and down a long hallway. I can't make out too much of the house since every door we pass is closed. The Castells certainly like their privacy, and since at least Victor knew I was coming today, I have to assume the closed doors are to keep me out.

He stops at the room at the very end of the hallway, and oddly enough it's the only door that isn't shut. "Most of Veronica's things are at her apartment off-campus, but you are welcome to look around." He motions for us to step inside. "I'll join you after I check on my wife. This has all been very hard on her."

Dad nods to Victor, but I'm already inside the room, taking in every aspect. The walls are a pale pink, more reminiscent of a child's room than a college coed's. The large bed in the middle has sheer white curtains surrounding it and more pillows than I've owned in my entire life. The dresser, desk, and bookshelves are all pristine white wood. It doesn't appear as if anyone actually lives in the room. It's almost like a shrine. A perfectly kept room that you'd expect parents not to disturb after a child dies at an early age.

"Anyone else find this a little too neat?" Detective Brennan asks, dragging a finger across the top of the bookshelf by the back window.

"And disturbing," I add, astonished that I'm agreeing with him for once. "They must have a cleaning service. No college student is this neat." I step toward the bed, pushing back the white curtain. I'm afraid of the things I'll see if I touch the bed, but nothing else in this room screams personal effect. It's all so...staged and impersonal.

I reach my hand out tentatively toward the closest pillow. "Okay, Veronica, let's see what you've seen."

CHAPTER FOUR

Veronica twirls a lock of chestnut brown hair around her index finger as she stares up at the canopy over her bed. "Will, I already told you. I can't come back tonight. It's my father's birthday. The whole reason I came home in the first place."

"You promised, V. What am I supposed to tell the guys?" The voice on the other end of the line is strained—almost a mixture of disappointment and anger.

"I'm sure you can find someone else to do it."

Will scoffs. "Sure. Find someone else who would be willing to serve drinks at our rush party and then do a pole dance for everyone afterward? No one else moves like you do, baby."

Veronica smiles. "That's true, but I still can't do it. Not tonight. I'll make it up to you, though."

"How?"

Veronica flips over on the bed and runs a finger down the center of the pillow her head was just using. "You know how."

"I like it when you talk dirty to me."

"I'm not having phone sex with you when my parents are in the next room." Her words don't match the look of pleasure on her face.

"Please, your house is a mansion. The next room is miles away." He pauses before adding. *"Besides, you owe me."*

Veronica's smile quickly fades. "I don't owe you anything. God, you sure do know how to kill the mood."

"You're a tease, V. You know that? A goddamn tease!"

"Go screw yourself, Will, because no one else is going to." She ends the call and tosses her phone to the foot of the bed. *"Bastard!"*

When I open my eyes, I nearly jump backward. Detective Brennan is standing on the other side of the bed with a strange smile on his face.

"I'm guessing you saw something good, judging by the faces you made." He smirks and takes a seat on the bed. "Care to tell me what kinky things have transpired here?"

I take a deep breath to control myself. "All I saw was an argument between Veronica and some frat guy named Will."

"Then why did you look so...turned on?" At least Brennan has the decency to lower his voice.

"I wasn't." Veronica was. Before she got completely annoyed with Will. "And I'd prefer if you were nowhere near me when I'm having a vision."

Brennan raises his hands. "Didn't mean to offend you. Sheesh, Piper, maybe you need a little action to get you to loosen up." He moves the curtain and stands up.

I take another deep breath before turning to face my father, who must have heard our conversation judging by how close he's standing to the bed. "Nothing useful. Just a first name: Will."

25

Dad nods. "We'll ask Victor Castell for a list of Veronica's college friends."

"I need to see her car. If that was the last known place she was, that's where I'll pick up on the most information that's actually useful to the case." I start for the door and come face-to-face with Victor Castell.

"Finished already?" he asks me. "Did you find anything? Do you know where she is yet?"

Wow, he thinks I'm a miracle worker, and his wife thinks I'm a quack. Great combo. Neither is correct.

"I need to see Veronica's car. Is it here?"

"Yes. The police already dusted it for fingerprints, though." Victor starts down the hallway with us on his heels. "She didn't have much in the car since she only came home for a night."

I don't need the effects inside the car. I need the car itself. "That won't be a problem, Mr. Castell."

We pass Darla on our way through the kitchen to the garage. She levels me with a look and shakes her head before sipping her tea, which is steaming. By the smell, I know she's drinking green tea. I smile at her, not being able to resist the opportunity to make her feel more uncomfortable. I know I should cut her some slack since her daughter is missing, but I'm so tired of people judging me the second they find out what I do for a living. As if I asked for these abilities. Here I am trying to do something useful with them, trying to save people, and I'm still looked at like a freak.

Dad holds the garage door open for me, giving me his "Behave" look as I pass through. He knows me too well.

The Castells have a six-car garage full of Mercedes, BMWs, and a Lexus. Victor leads us to the Lexus.

"Damn," Detective Brennan says. "When I was in college, I drove a beat-up Honda Civic." He runs his hand across the pristine black paint as he walks around the hood. "This is a Lexus LS 460 F Sport, isn't it?"

"You know your cars," Victor says.

"It's a beauty." Brennan leans down and peers inside the window.

I roll my eyes and grip the door handle. "Excuse me," I say, waiting for him to move so I can open the door.

Brennan doesn't even notice my annoyance. He steps aside, opens the back door, and immediately sits down. "There are adjustable back seats with foot rests."

I flash him a look and say, "Need I remind you we are looking for a missing girl, not car shopping?"

"Sorry." He busies himself looking around the back seat.

I slip into the driver's seat, resting my hands on the wood trimmed steering wheel. I expect to sense Veronica, but instead all that comes to my mind is leather. I shake my head. *I need more than that. Come on.* I squeeze the steering wheel tighter in my hands. The feel of soft leather wraps itself around my fingers. Gloves.

I open my eyes and turn to Victor Castell. "Does Veronica wear leather driving gloves?"

"No. Not that I know of."

I center myself again, allowing my senses to fill. But again all I get is leather gloves. "What time did Veronica leave your house on Saturday?"

"Right after dinner, so around eight. Maybe eight thirty." Victor doesn't sound sure at all and I'd love to read his expression, but I'm focusing on reading this steering wheel.

Show me something. Anything else. My hand lowers to the seat adjuster, and I don't realize I'm doing it until the

27

seat slides back and Brennan says, "Hey! Watch it. I have my feet up back here."

I'm used to my visions being unclear at times—most of the time, even. But this is odd. I can't sense anything other than hands wearing leather gloves. "Brown leather gloves."

"Excuse me?" Victor says.

I let go of the steering wheel and look up at him. "I'm sensing brown leather gloves."

"That's impossible. Veronica hates the color brown. She'd never wear brown gloves." He holds up a finger. "Although, she did buy me a pair of brown leather gloves for my birthday last year."

Dad's eyes flash between mine and the back of Victor Castell's head. His right hand moves to his hip, where I know his gun is holstered under his jacket. He thinks Victor is responsible for his daughter's kidnapping. It doesn't feel right to me, though.

I give an almost imperceptible shake of my head, which makes Dad lower his hand again, though he keeps his gaze locked on Victor from his place at the front of the car.

"Why would you see something from so long ago?" Victor asks me.

"I'm not sure. Unfortunately, I can't control what I see. It's possible Veronica was thinking about the gift while she was driving."

"That would make sense," Victor says. "She bought me a driving hat this year to match the gloves. I could show it to you if you think it would help."

"That won't be necessary," I say.

Dad and Detective Brennan do a thorough search of the vehicle, Dad doing most of the actual police work, including checking out the flat tire, while Brennan oohed and aahed over the many bells and whistles the car offers.

I can't stop focusing on the steering wheel. It's over-whelming my thoughts. But why? Was Veronica heading somewhere other than back to school?

"Mr. Castell?" I ask, interrupting a conversation about the base price of such a vehicle. What college coed drives a car that starts at eighty grand?

"Yes?" Every time he looks at me, it's with such hope in his eyes.

I lower my gaze. "Where was Veronica going?"

"Back to school of course."

"The University of Pennsylvania?" I ask, not sure why I know that but certain I'm correct. I'm also sure that Castell bought his daughter into the Ivy League university.

"That's correct. It's about a three-hour drive from here."

"Where was her car found?"

"Not far away, actually. Veronica likes to take back roads. She hates traffic."

Yet she goes to college in Philadelphia. "Did she grow up here?"

"Yes. There was construction on the road where the car was found. She must have run over some metal that wound up in the road. Her tire was punctured, and whatever it was that she hit, didn't stay in the wheel." He motions me to the rear driver's side tire and bends down next to it. He points to a large gash. "See, right here is where the—"

"I'm assuming the road was searched," I interrupt, running my fingers over the tear in the rubber. My eyes close, and I see a hunting knife with a black handle. And leather driving gloves.

Veronica Castell didn't get a flat tire. Someone wearing brown leather driving gloves slashed her tire with a hunting knife and then drove her car.

CHAPTER FIVE

"Are you sure about this?" Dad asks me at dinner that night.

I didn't want to mention my latest vision in front of Mr. Castell, on the off chance that I was wrong about him and he is responsible for his daughter's disappearance. "I'm not sure about much, but this...yes."

"Do you really think he'd kidnap his own daughter?" Mom asks, placing the pot roast on the table between the garlic mashed potatoes and cooked baby carrots. They have me over for dinner once a week since I hate cooking meals for myself. My dinners usually consist of a bowl of cereal or French fries and a Frosty from the Wendy's drive-through. Feeding me once a week is Mom's way of making sure I don't die of malnutrition.

"You should have told me all this before we left his house. I could have demanded to see the gloves so you could properly ID them." Dad takes a large gulp of his iced tea.

"We both know me IDing a pair of gloves isn't going to be enough to pin this on Victor Castell." I scoop some carrots onto my plate and raise my brow at Dad, who holds his empty plate out to me. I dish some for him and then

30

Mom. "I think I'd know if it was him. I only saw him clearly in one vision, and it was obvious he loves his daughter."

"I could have at least asked him if he owns a hunting knife. We left too many stones unturned, Piper. This isn't like you." Dad takes a heaping forkful of mashed potatoes and puts it in his mouth.

"You saw the way his wife glared at me. What do you think she would have done if I accused her husband of this crime and got him arrested? She'd be telling the world I'm a fraud and demanding my license." I'm not about to risk my career at the hands of a nonbeliever. I need concrete evidence, and right now, I have none.

"So, what now?" Mom asks, trying to be the voice of reason as always when Dad and I argue over a case.

"I need to see the place where Veronica's car 'broke down.'" I make air quotes before picking up my fork and stabbing a piece of pot roast. "I don't think Veronica was the one driving her car that night."

"Were any of her friends home from college?" Dad asks as if Mom or I would know.

I shrug. "Would you mind calling the Castells tomorrow to find out?"

"Will do. I'll get the exact location of the car from the police report, and we'll head there first thing in the morning." He points his fork at the mashed potatoes. "You did something different with these," he says, looking at Mom.

She smiles. "My little secret. Do you like them?"

Dad nods and sticks another forkful in his mouth.

"Can we leave the junior detective home this time?" I ask.

"Mitchell?" Mom narrows her brow at me. "He seems like such a nice boy. Smart, too."

More like a smartass. "How did you get stuck with him as your partner anyway?" I ask Dad. "You never told me."

Dad laughs. "He requested it. I think it's because he wanted to work with you."

I nearly choke on my iced tea.

"Too much lemon?" Mom asks with a knowing smile.

"Very funny."

She laughs. "Say what you will, but I've always said that man has his eye on you." She winks at me.

"Please, Mom. I'm trying to eat here."

"Mitchell—"

"Detective Brennan," I correct her, "is a pompous ass."

"Whatever you say, dear." Mom suppresses a smile and pops a carrot into her mouth.

Dad meets my gaze and shrugs. "I will say he's fascinated by what you do, Piper."

"That's the problem. It's hard to concentrate when he's leering at me. He's not much better than Darla Castell."

"He's a good detective, though. You have to give him that."

"We'll see tomorrow when we check out the crime scene."

———

I opt to meet Dad and Detective Brennan the next morning, driving my Mazda to Keystone Drive, a back road surrounded by nothing but trees on both sides. According to the police report, Veronica's car was found near a cell tower that was recently erected—the source of the so-called metal object they thought punctured her tire. I pull off the road onto the grass about fifty feet north of the cell tower.

I could wait for Dad and Brennan, but if I'm going to have a vision, I'd rather do it without Brennan eyeing me like I'm a circus act. I step out of my car, looking around on the ground for any debris from the cell tower construction. As I predicted, there is none. Though it could just mean it was cleared by the police to keep anyone else from breaking down.

I search the road for tire tracks or anything out of the ordinary. I keep walking north, but nothing catches my eye, so I start back toward my car. I try to remember Veronica's tire. The rim was bent, meaning she drove on the tire after it was slashed with that knife. That could mean she went further south before stopping. The part that bothered me the most is how she didn't realize she was driving on a flat tire until she got to this point. A slashed tire doesn't leak as slowly as one punctured by a nail or something small like that.

I follow the road around a blind corner and nearly have a heart attack when a car speeds down the road behind me, swerving at the last second before hitting me. I jump into the grass, falling over a large divot in the ground. Brake lights come on, and the car pulls off the road. "You've got to be kidding me." I watch Detective Brennan get out of the driver's seat, his eyes landing on me.

"Are you crazy? What are you doing walking in the road?" he asks like it's my fault he almost killed me.

"Piper, are you okay?" Dad rushes over to me and offers a hand to help me up.

"Fine." I wipe the dirt from the back of my jeans. "Speed Racer over here needs to learn to drive."

"You were in the middle of the road."

"I was not. There's no shoulder on the turn."

"Okay!" Dad holds up his hands to silence us. "That's

enough. If you two can't work together..." His eyes meet mine, and then he turns to Brennan. "Mitchell, you're a good kid, but this is my daughter."

"Right." Brennan nods and puts his hands on his hips in defiance. "So in other words, I play nice or you request a new partner."

Dad would do it, too. For me. But I don't want him getting in trouble for my sake. "No one is going anywhere." I inhale, counting to eight before releasing. My right hand has a layer of dirt and gravel on it from what I wiped off my jeans. "You're—"

Brakes squeal as the Lexus jerks to a stop on the side of the road. The driver's side door opens and gravel crunches under heavy boots. It's too dark to make out any features, but the figure bends down and plunges the hunting knife into the rear tire. Then he or she moves back to the car and adjusts the front seat, moving it forward.

"I'm what?" Detective Brennan says, his voice laced with anger. "Damn it, Piper! What the—? Oh." His tone softens as he realizes what just happened.

I rub my temple. This is too strange. "I don't even think Veronica was in the car when it was left here."

"Left here?" Dad asks. "You mean when she went to get help?"

That was the theory the police had. That Veronica got a flat and walked to find a gas station or someone to help. But that can't be what happened. "She'd call for help, not walk." A girl like Veronica Castell wouldn't walk three miles to get someone to change her tire.

Dad shakes his head. "The cell tower isn't fully functional yet. They haven't finished working on it. Reception is spotty at best. She'd have to start walking if she hoped to get a signal."

I pull my phone out of my back pocket, noticing the screen protector is shattered from when I fell on my ass earlier. I pull it off so I can actually read the display and pocket it in my jacket to dispose of later. I press Dad's number and wait. His phone doesn't ring, so I hold the phone to my ear. "It's ringing on my end."

"So you have a connection, but your dad doesn't?" Detective Brennan asks. He removes his phone and checks the signal. "Nothing for me either."

I end the call when Dad's voice mail picks up. "So whether or not you have reception here depends on which cell carrier you use." Cell service is the one thing I don't skimp on. I use the best carrier in the area. Dad, on the other hand, insists they're all the same and doesn't believe in paying more for one than another. "I'm sure Veronica has the most expensive cell carrier and plan known to man. If I'm getting service, I'm willing to bet she did, too."

"We'll check her phone records again, but something would have come up by now if she did make a call." Dad sighs and looks around. "What happened to you, Veronica?" he calls out.

More importantly, who is the person with the leather gloves and hunting knife? "Why would someone move the driver's seat after slashing the tire?" I ask, my eyes on Dad, but it's Brennan who answers.

"If it wasn't Veronica driving the car, but the person wanted to make it look like it had been, they'd adjust the seat to her size before leaving."

"That's true," I say. "So, maybe my feeling is right. Maybe Veronica wasn't even in the car when it was abandoned here."

"Then where was she?" Dad asks.

"I think that's the real question we need to answer."

CHAPTER SIX

"How was the book?" Marcia asks, meeting me at the bakery counter.

"Great, actually." I stayed up until midnight, reading the entire book in one sitting. Lately, reading is my only escape from cases.

"I figured you finished it since I didn't see you in here at eight o'clock for your morning coffee." She pours me a to-go cup of toasted almond, knowing that's why I'm here.

"I had an early morning on the job. I'm just heading to the office now." I take out my phone and set it next to the register. "Can I get a blueberry muffin? Oh, and I need to pay for that book and grab one of the other new ones you got in."

Marcia pulls a book out from behind the register. "I put it here yesterday after I scanned it into the system. I saw you eyeing it. You could have taken it, you know."

She's such a sweetheart. "I wouldn't have gotten any sleep if I had this one to read, too," I joke.

She places my bagged blueberry muffin, book, and coffee on the counter. "Anything else?"

"Nope. That should do it."

The bell on the door jingles, and Marcia looks up with a smile. "Hello, Detective."

I turn, expecting to see Dad, but Detective Brennan walks over.

"Marcia, you're looking as beautiful as ever."

I roll my eyes and use my phone to pay my bill.

"No need to sweet talk me, Detective."

I smile at Marcia, who's had to listen to me complain about Brennan on more than one occasion.

"I suppose you're used to compliments," Detective Brennan says, flashing his perfectly white teeth.

I lean against the glass counter, not willing to leave poor Marcia to deal with Brennan on her own. "She does have the right to refuse service to anyone, you know. So I'd try to keep the bullshitting to a minimum before she kicks your ass out of here."

Detective Brennan jerks his thumb in my direction and addresses Marcia. "This one. I have no words for her."

"Oh, I have plenty," Marcia says. "Independent, tough, smart, talented..." She places her hand on top of mine. "Not to mention she's a great friend."

Detective Brennan takes a step back. "Okay, I see I'm outnumbered here. How about I just place my order and get on with my day?"

"Now you're talking. What can I get you, Detective?" Marcia steps toward the coffee pot, anticipating his answer.

"Light and sweet, please," he says. He motions to my bag. "What did you get?"

"The last blueberry muffin. Too bad for you." I give him a mocking pout.

"I don't care for blueberries." He scrunches up his nose

before addressing Marcia. "Do you have banana nut muffins?"

"Sure do." Marcia puts the coffee on the counter and bags the muffin.

"Nothing better to do, Piper?" Brennan asks me, pulling his credit card from his wallet. "Or are you waiting for me?"

"Actually, I'm here for moral support for Marcia. You know, in case you drive her crazy and I need to physically remove you from the store."

He eyes me. "Physically remove me? That I'd like to see."

Marcia rings up his order, and he swipes his card.

"Tips are appreciated," I tell him, motioning to the tip jar.

He reaches into his wallet, pulls out a twenty, and deposits it in the jar. My mouth nearly drops open. What is he trying to prove?

"Thank you, Detective," Marcia says, also in shock. "Come back anytime." She looks to me, but I'm speechless.

"Piper, may I walk you out? I have a few things I want to run by you for the case." Detective Brennan motions to the door.

"How did I know I wasn't getting rid of you that easily?"

"Like Marcia said, you're smart." He smiles and takes a sip of his coffee. His lips purse, and he stamps his foot on the floor. "Hot!" he says, after forcing the coffee down his throat.

I look at Marcia. "Apparently, I have to be smart enough for the both of us since we're working together."

"Lucky you," Marcia says with a laugh. She waves as we walk out of the store.

"What's her deal?" Brennan asks once we reach my office.

I pull my keys from my purse, but instead of unlocking the door, I glare at him. "She's so far out of your league it's laughable."

"Fine. Other fish in the sea." He sips his coffee.

"Why are you such a jerk?" I ask, opening the door and turning on the lights.

"Why are you such a bitch?" he counters.

I smirk as I walk to my desk and put my purse and book in the bottom drawer. I drop the muffin bag on the desk next to my laptop. "My father says you requested to work with him. Why?" I take a large sip of coffee, letting the flavor wash over my tongue.

"The real answer?"

"If you think you can handle giving an honest answer for once."

"See, that's where you're wrong about me, Piper." He sits down in the chair opposite mine, draping one foot on top of the other knee and tossing his muffin bag on the desk. "I'm too honest for you. I tell it like it is, and you hate that."

"Really?" I sit down, determined not to let him see that he gets to me. I lean back in the leather chair, holding my coffee cup in both hands. "Go on. Psychoanalyze me. I'd love to hear this."

"I'm confident. Some would say sure of myself. You, on the other hand, doubt yourself, which I guess is understandable considering you see these things that you can't make sense of. People come to you to solve their problems, find their loved ones, and each time you question yourself. That's got to be rough."

I nod, biting the inside of my lower lip. He's smarter than I've given him credit for. "Okay, so you figured you'd volunteer to be my father's partner so you could get an inside peek at the unstable psychic. Is that it?"

"No." He sits forward, lowering his foot to the floor and placing his coffee on the desk. "I know what you're capable of, and I'm impressed. I think I believe in you more than you believe in yourself."

I laugh. "Sure." I bring the coffee cup to my lips, but he reaches forward and grabs it, lowering it.

"Stop hiding behind sarcasm."

"I'm not—"

"Yes, you are. You do it all the time."

I jerk my cup from his hand. "Because you know me so well? We just started working together. Before that, I only saw you a handful of times. Granted a handful too many—"

"And there it is again!" He throws his hand in the air. "You know what I think?"

"I'm sure I don't. I don't speak lunatic."

He laughs. "You're just proving my point more and more every time you open your mouth."

I clamp my lips shut, letting my eyes say everything for me.

"The only people you let in are your parents and Marcia. You never even gave me a chance."

"A chance for what?" I ask.

"To be your friend."

I scoff. "Please. What woman have you ever been friends with? I see the way you hit on everything in heels."

"I like women. Sue me. That doesn't mean I'm incapable of being friends with one."

"You hate me just as much as I hate you. For someone who swears he's so honest, I'd think you'd have the common decency to admit that." I take another sip of my coffee, which is already getting too cold for my liking. I continue to gulp it down until it's finished.

"You really think I hate you?" His voice softens.

"You've done nothing but insult me ever since we met. I think your male ego can't handle me because you know you can't flatter me like you do other women." I toss the empty cup in the garbage, which is already half-full with paper coffee cups.

Brennan laces his fingers in his lap. "I'm not going to apologize for who I am, Piper. At least I'm willing to work together and—"

I sit up straight. "Your interest in working with me lies solely in wanting to see my psychic abilities in action. Do you think I don't notice the way you look at me when I'm having a vision? You stare at me like I'm a sideshow. You're mocking what I do. That's why you're here."

Brennan stares at his fingernails, and for a moment, I don't even think he's heard a word I said. "My mother was psychic."

"What?" This has to be a trick.

He nods. "She didn't try to use her abilities. Not at all, actually. But I remember there were times when she knew things were going to happen before they happened."

"She was clairvoyant?"

He stops studying his fingernails, but he still won't look at me. "She never claimed to be, and I don't really know if you'd call it that. I just remember a few times..." He lets out a deep breath. "My brother and I were playing basketball in the driveway one day. I was twelve, and my brother was ten. Mom came racing out the front door, yelling that there was a loose dog. She screamed for us to get in the house. We did, and seconds later, this dog came tearing into our driveway, snarling and foaming at the mouth. It was rabid. According to the biopsy, it had been bitten by a rabid raccoon. At first I thought my mom had seen the dog on the news or heard about it from a neighbor, but later she admitted to my dad that she saw the entire thing happen."

"You mean she saw it in her mind," I say.

He nods. "She didn't know I overheard their conversation. But a few years later, she was supposed to go visit her sister in California. Her sister had a baby and Dad couldn't take off work, so Mom planned to go on her own. My brother and I begged her to let us go with her, but she said we couldn't miss school." He stops talking and swallows hard.

He's been talking about his mother in the past tense since he brought her up, so I have a pretty good idea of where this is going. "You don't have to tell me," I say.

He closes his eyes. "She called us from the plane. Said she loved us. She was crying, and I remember feeling like she was saying goodbye."

"Oh my God." She saw her own death. I can't even imagine what that would be like.

"I'm sure she knew the plane was going to crash."

I reach forward, placing my hand on his forearm.

"I love you, Mitchell. You take care of Nicholas, okay? And be good for your father."

"Mom, are you okay?" Mitchell's voice shakes, and he grips the phone tightly, pressing it to his face.

"Don't you worry about me, sweetheart. You just take care of yourself and your brother. Promise me."

"Did you...see something?"

"No. Don't talk like that, baby. I love you. I have to go now."

"No, Mom. Don't go! Mom! Talk to me! Mom!"

When the vision fades, I realize I'm crying. I let go of Mitchell—Detective Brennan—and swipe at my eyes. I spin the chair so I'm facing the windows looking out on Fifth Street.

"Did you just...?" Brennan asks.

"Yeah." I take a deep breath and blink back the remaining dampness in my eyes before facing him again. "I'm sorry. I didn't mean for that to happen."

"Is that why you push people away? Because you're afraid you'll see things about them?"

I'm not ready to have this conversation. Not with Brennan. Not even after what I saw. "You wanted to talk to me about the case, right?"

"Piper." He leans forward, and I get up, needing to put distance between us.

"I think it's best if we just focus on the case. Veronica's case is no closer to being solved, and we might be running out of time." There hasn't been a ransom letter, which means this might not be about money after all. Someone might just want to hurt Veronica. Someone like Will from the University of Pennsylvania. "There's someone we need to look into. The person I heard in my vision. He wanted Veronica to come back to school early. They fought about it."

Detective Brennan studies me for a moment before slumping back in his seat. "I guess it's worth looking into."

"It won't be easy since all I know is his name is Will and he's in a fraternity."

"Can't make those visions any clearer, huh?" He means it as a joke, but we both know there's truth behind it.

"Maybe I should check out the car again. I have to be missing something." I tilt my head back, focusing on the white of the ceiling. Sometimes staring at a blank space helps me clear my mind.

"I'm up for that. I'll put in a call to the Castells."

"I can handle it myself," I say.

He huffs and stands up, forcing my attention back to him. "You don't get it. We're partners, whether you like it or not. If you're checking out the car again, then so am I." His jaw clenches, and his nostrils flare. "My mother wouldn't talk to us about her visions, and look where it got her. Do you really think I'm going to stand by and watch the same thing happen to you?"

"Brennan—"

He waves his hand in the air. "Don't. I'll call you with a time to go to the Castells'." He storms out of my office.

I stare out the window after him as he walks down the street to his car, which is parked on the other side of Marcia's Nook. Detective Brennan requested to be my father's partner for one reason. He couldn't save his mother from the visions she had, so he wants to try to save me.

CHAPTER SEVEN

"Thank you for seeing us again on such short notice," I say when Victor Castell greets us at the front door of his home. He looks worse than he did yesterday. Dark circles line his eyes, and his clothes are rumpled like he slept in them.

"Of course. Anything that will speed up the search for my daughter. Please come inside."

"Actually, we'd like to see Veronica's car again if you don't mind," Detective Brennan says.

"You know the way," Victor says. "There's something I need to get. I'll meet you in the garage."

We nod and walk toward the garage.

"What do you think that was about?" Brennan asks me.

"No clue." I hurry through the kitchen and to the garage door. This time, the Mercedes is missing. "I guess Darla is out," I say. *Good riddance.*

"I'm sure you're relieved."

I flash him a look but quickly regret it. I spent the last four hours thinking about his mother and what I saw in that vision. I'm sure he initially just wanted to learn more about my abilities as a way to understand his mother's. But when he actually witnessed me having a few visions, something changed in him. Maybe it was seeing how they could be so clear one moment and so vague the next. Maybe he was trying to figure out how awful his mother's final vision had been.

The truth is, the ability his mother had isn't the same as mine. I typically read the energy off objects or people. I don't see the future, or I might be able to stop these missing persons cases from ever becoming cases to begin with.

"Piper? Are you having a vision?" Brennan asks, and I realize I've been staring at the Lexus.

"No. Sorry. Just a normal, everyday zoning out. I was up late reading, and now I'm paying the price."

"Even after all that coffee?"

"Caffeine doesn't exactly wake me up." I've developed a tolerance for it after consuming it in massive amounts.

"Look, about what I said in your office—"

I shake my head. "It's fine. I get it. But you have to understand I'm not your mother."

He laughs. "Considering you're two years younger than I am, that would be a physical impossibility."

"You know what I mean."

"I do. And I know helping you isn't going to change what happened to her, but I still want to. Help you, that is. My mom hid her ability. You're using yours to help other people, and I admire that."

"Did you just pay me a genuine compliment?" I can't resist teasing him.

"Don't let it go to your head. Besides, you're not that good or you would have solved this case already."

I cock my head at him. "Ah, there's the jerk I've come to tolerate."

He holds a hand to his chest and bats his eyes. "Tolerate. You know how to melt a man's heart."

The inside garage door opens before I can come back with a witty response. Victor Castell walks toward us, leather driving gloves in his hand. He holds them out to me.

"I wanted to show these to you. These are the gloves Veronica bought for me." He swallows hard at the mention of his daughter's name. "I'm not hiding anything, Ms. Ashwell. I'm certain these aren't the same gloves you saw in your vision." He places them in my outstretched hand.

Detective Brennan raises a questioning brow at me.

The gloves look similar, but they're not an exact match.

"Darling, come look at the beautiful driving gloves Veronica gave me." Victor holds up the gloves for Darla to see.

"Very nice, dear, but you have a driver. Whatever do you need driving gloves for?"

Veronica's face falls. "Daddy, you hired a driver?"

"Oh, sweetie," Darla says, reaching for her daughter. "I'm so sorry. It's a lovely gift and very thoughtful of you. You had no way of knowing your father hired a driver."

Victor wraps his arms around Veronica and kisses the side of her head. "Your mother is right. Besides, any man would love to have gloves as stylish as these."

"Ms. Ashwell," Victor says.

I look back and forth between him and Brennan. "They aren't a match." I hand them back to Victor, who nods and walks back into the house.

"Poor guy," Detective Brennan says.

"Yeah. He definitely didn't do anything to his daughter."

"What did you see?"

I give him a sideways glance before opening the driver's

side door of Veronica's Lexus. "Just Veronica giving her father the gloves."

"What's it like? I mean, do you just see the events like you're watching a movie, or do you almost experience them like you're part of what's happening?"

I'm afraid to answer his question because I know he's still trying to figure out his mother's abilities. "It depends. Most of the time, I see them like a movie."

"And the other times?" He grips the car door, his eyes focused on me. "I can handle it, you know. Remember, I'm the cocky asshole you love to make feel bad, so lay it on me."

"I don't—"

He holds up a hand. "Just tell me."

"Other times, I feel things without seeing them. Or hear things. Smell things. Taste things."

"So really any of the senses."

I nod and reach for the steering wheel.

"Why are you so fixated on that? What about the rest of the car?"

"I don't know. Something about it is telling me to focus on it. I can't explain it." God, I must sound like a freak, talking about objects speaking to me. I try to dismiss the thought and focus on the car again.

"But you're seeing the same things, right? You know the definition of crazy?"

"Doing the same thing over and over again and expecting different results?"

He answers with a smile. "I do believe I just got you to insult yourself."

"You're so talented." I feel at ease falling into our usual banter. I grip the steering wheel, but this time nothing happens. No visions. No feelings. Nothing. I reach for the seat controls since I know the person who slashed the tires did the same. Again nothing. "This isn't working." I lean my head back against the seat.

Detective Brennan's hand wraps around my wrist, and he gently tugs me from the car. "Come on."

"And do what?" I stare at him, waiting for some brilliant answer to my question.

"I don't know, but you have to try something different. No steering wheel, seat, or tire." He looks around at the rest of the car. "What about the trunk? Veronica probably had a suitcase or bag in there, right? She didn't come home for the night without bringing anything with her."

"I guess." I start for the trunk, hoping we'll find a bag, because an empty trunk isn't likely to give me much to read. "Can you find a trunk latch in the driver's seat?"

He sticks his head in the car, and a few seconds later, the trunk pops up an inch. I stick my hand in and lift the trunk.

"Damn it!" I smack the side of the car.

Detective Brennan walks around and joins me. He reaches inside the trunk and lifts up the bottom to reveal a spare tire. "Not surprised Veronica didn't know how to change the tire herself."

"It does support my theory that she would have called someone to help her, though. She had the spare tire right here. She just needed someone to put it on for her."

"Your dad is combing through the phone records and hunting down Veronica's friend Will. He should have something for us by now if you want to call this a wash and head to the station."

I stare at the car, convinced I'm missing something. "She was in this car. There should be something here to help me."

"You mean to help *us*."

I level him with a look. "Unless you're having visions all of a sudden, I mean *me*."

"You're not alone, though. Let's think this through. You don't think Veronica was driving the car."

"No, I don't."

"So why have you only checked the driver's seat?"

I smack my open palm to my forehead. "You're right." I walk around to the passenger seat but stop before opening the door.

"What's wrong?"

"I didn't see Veronica in the passenger seat either."

Brennan furrows his brow. "Okay, so maybe Veronica was taken somewhere before the car was dumped on Keystone. That means she could have been in the passenger seat before that."

I shake my head. "No. She was in the back."

He jerks his head back. "How do you know?"

"I just do. It's one of those things I can't explain." I reach for the rear door, but Brennan grabs it first, opening it for me. I give him a quizzical look. "Are you trying to be a gentleman, or do you not get how my visions work?"

"Neither. You're moving way too slowly for me."

I've never wanted to roll my eyes as much as I have since meeting him. "I have to physically touch things to see what happened." I reach for the door again, placing my hand on the latch. "See. Touching."

"You are not easy to work with."

"Finally, something we have in common." I close my eyes, clearing my mind and waiting to see something.

"Anything?"

I open one eye and peer at him. "Silence helps."

He clamps his mouth shut, and I close my eye again.

Come on, Veronica. Where are you?

50

No vision comes. "Damn it!" I open my eyes and get in the car, lying across the back seat like I imagine Veronica would have if someone tied her up.

"Do you need help?" Brennan asks. "I could handcuff you if you'd like."

"I think you'd like that a little too much."

He smirks and reaches for the cuffs.

I raise my boot, which is level with a very sensitive area of his body. "I'd rethink that if I were you."

"Well played." He nods and steps away from the car.

I stare at the ceiling, trying to concentrate, but all I can think is this car is more comfortable than my bed. "I might fall asleep in here."

"It's amazing, isn't it? Luxury reclining back seats. If my parents had this car when I was growing up, I wouldn't have complained when Mom made us sit in the car for hours on end driving to Florida." His face falls, making me wonder if that was the last trip he ever took with his mother.

Since I'm not getting any visions, I sit up and get out of the car. "Speaking of parents, let's go meet up with my dad. I'm not getting anything else from this car."

"Please tell me it's Ashwell family dinner night," Brennan says as we walk back toward the kitchen.

"Nope. That was last night, and it's family only."

"Damn. No chance of me scoring an invite then."

"Not unless you plan on marrying my parents' dog. I should warn you Max's favorite past times are sniffing his ass and bathing himself in front of company."

"Ah, he and I have that in common." He nudges my side with his elbow.

"Dear God, you're like the older brother I never wanted, aren't you?"

"More like the second cousin twice removed."

"I'm not sure I ever understood what that meant."

"Me neither. Just sounds good."

"Why are they here again?" Darla Castell's voice comes through the door before we leave the garage.

"They needed to see Veronica's car again," Victor says. "They're doing everything they can to find her."

"It doesn't seem that way. I mean, why on earth did you have to show them your gloves. They can't possibly think you had anything to do with this." She sniffles and then coughs.

Not wanting to intrude on their private conversation, I stomp my feet to announce our arrival and open the door. Darla's head whips in our direction. She opens her mouth to speak but then flees the room instead.

"Thank you for your time, Mr. Castell," Detective Brennan says. "We are following up on two possible leads, and we'll be in touch as soon as we know anything."

Victor's eyes go to me, assuming the leads are mine. I nod in agreement.

"Thank you both." He shakes our hands and walks us to the front door.

Brennan drives in the direction of the station, where we're meeting Dad, but halfway there I get an idea. "Turn right here," I say, tugging on the steering wheel.

"Whoa! What do you think you're doing?"

"Making your wish come true." I press my parents' number and put my phone to my ear.

"Sweetheart, you have no idea what my wish is."

I glare at him and cover the speaker on my phone. "Can you not revert to a sexist pig, please? I'm scoring you an invite to dinner."

He smiles and motions for me to carry on.

"Hello?"

"Hey, Mom."

"Piper, how are you?"

"Fine, but I need to have a business dinner with Dad. Any chance you have room for two more at the table tonight?"

"Does this mean you're bringing Mitchell Brennan?" Her tone isn't lost on me. Mom has been trying to get me to date for years. It's not that I'm not attracted to anyone. It's just that dating is overwhelming for me. Seeing your boyfriend's previous sexual partners in the heat of the moment is too much to handle. So until I can learn to block my visions, I can't get that close to anyone.

"Piper?" Mom says when I don't respond.

"He is Dad's partner, so he kind of needs to be there. Is that okay?"

"Of course. I made meatloaf. There's plenty to go around."

"Great. See you in ten." I hang up and dial Dad, filling him in on the change of plans.

"You didn't have to do that," Brennan says.

I shrug. "It's no big deal. I'm guessing your family doesn't live in the area."

"Nope. They live in North Carolina, near Asheville. I see them at Christmas and usually once over the summer. My younger brother, Nicholas, is married with his first child on the way."

I nod, not sure how to respond. Marriage and kids aren't something I see in my future. I doubt Brennan sees them in his future either. As much as I don't want to admit it, he and I might be more alike than I thought.

CHAPTER EIGHT

Dad wipes his mouth with a napkin before standing up. "Dinner was delicious, Bonnie. Thank you."

Mom smiles as she begins clearing the plates from the table. I stand up and reach for a plate, but she holds her hand up. "You three have spared me the details of this case all through dinner. I know you have work to do, so go in the living room and get to it. I can handle loading the dishwasher on my own."

"Thank you, Mrs. Ashwell," Brennan says. "And I'll second how delicious dinner was. I can't remember the last time I ate a home-cooked meal."

Mom cocks her head. "You and Piper need to start eating better. What is it about single people not cooking?" She sighs and walks out with a stack of empty plates.

"Shall we?" Dad asks, motioning toward the living room.

Brennan and I follow him, Dad already launching into what he's been able to uncover. "So, there are plenty of fraternity boys named Will at the University of Pennsylvania." He sits down in the recliner in the corner. "Interviewing all of them would be extremely time-consuming." His gaze falls on me, and I know what he's asking: Is there any way for me to narrow the list without having to travel the three hours to UPenn?

"I'll do my best, Dad, but without more personal effects, this case is proving to be tougher than usual." I can't figure out why Veronica's presence seems to be missing from her car. If that was the last place she was known to be, I should get a ton of readings from it.

"I can drive down there if necessary," Detective Brennan says, addressing my father. "That way you and Piper can keep digging around here."

The problem with that is Brennan can't read people like I can. If I think one of the Wills is our guy, I could shake his hand and get a read off him. I'm like a human lie detector that way.

"What about phone records?" I ask Dad. "One of the numbers has to match one of the Wills."

"I had the same thought," Dad says. "The problem is that some of these college kids are still listed on their parents' phone plans. So the names don't necessarily match up."

"Last names would, though," Detective Brennan says.

"Unless the son was the product of another marriage—a stepson." The words don't register in my mind before they come out of my mouth. Which can only mean one thing. I said them because I know they're true. "That's it," I tell Dad. "He's the stepson, and he's on his stepfather's phone plan."

"Well that's just great." Brennan throws his hands in the air and then starts pacing the room. For a moment, I'm shocked he's not questioning how I know. But maybe since our heart-to-heart about his mom, he's resigned to accept my gut feelings.

"I feel like we're hitting road block after road block." I finally take a seat on the couch, leaning back against the arm and gazing out the window. I can't see much in the dark, even with the streetlights illuminating the road. Mom and Dad's neighborhood is quiet, not many children to run around even though it's unseasonably warm tonight, the high hitting around seventy.

"It's like someone went through a lot of trouble to cover their tracks." Brennan stops pacing, and I feel his eyes on me. "Is it possible that Veronica took off and tried to cover it up? Could she purposely throw off your visions?"

I run my fingers over the arm of the couch. "No. First, she had no way of knowing I'd be working this case. And second, if she tried to cover this up, I would see it for sure. My visions would show her doing it." Instead, my visions seem to be excluding her from the most important moments. Unless...

"We're assuming Veronica left after dinner, like Victor said." I stand up, needing to move around. I walk around the cherry wood coffee table and step toward the fireplace, even though it's not lit. "What if we're wrong? I can't sense Veronica in her car. So what if that means she never got in it to head back to school?" I turn to face Dad in his chair. "What if someone got to her before she could leave?"

"You mean kidnapped her in her own garage?" Brennan asks. "You would have picked up something when we were there, wouldn't you?"

I take a deep breath, trying to keep calm even though I'm exhausted at having to explain to people how my abilities work. If I read every object all the time, I'd go insane with voices and images bombarding my mind. When there are too many things around, I can tune them out. "I tend to focus on one thing at a time to get clearer readings."

"Like the steering wheel," Brennan says, moving toward me. "You were honed in on it, and I still don't know why."

"Because it wasn't Veronica who I read off it." That oddity had jumped out at me. My visions had let me know something was very wrong with this case.

"Okay, so I think we should go back to the Castells' again and scope out that garage. If she was taken before she even got to leave, there should be something there for you to—"

"Hang on." Dad holds his hand up and sits forward in his chair. He stares at me for a moment before continuing. "Pumpkin, Victor Castell called me today at the station. It was while you two"—he points back and forth between Brennan and me—"were at the house. He said his wife was having a really difficult time with detectives combing through their personal space. I think the incident with the driving gloves sent her into a panic."

"Because she thought I was accusing her husband of abducting their daughter," I say, giving Brennan a sideways glance since the accusation was actually made on his part. "I assured them that wasn't the case."

"I know, but he said his wife isn't comfortable with you working this case. She believes your presence is adding unnecessary stress to the situation."

"Unnecessary stress? Their daughter is missing! What the hell do they expect?"

Dad stands up and walks over to me, taking me by the shoulders. He dips his head so he's looking into my eyes.

"Mr. Castell was under the impression that you'd be able to tell them where his daughter is."

I laugh. "Just like that. The psychic swoops in and sees the missing daughter so the police can bring her home. They're living in a fairytale world." I turn away from him, facing the fireplace once again.

"So what now?" Brennan asks. "Do you and I go there without Piper?"

I whirl around, glaring at them both. "Just cut me out of the equation? You're really going to entertain this crazy notion?"

"Piper..." Dad doesn't know what else to say, which is saying all I need to know.

"Then I guess I should wish you both good luck." I storm past them, grabbing my purse from the coffee table. "Tell Mom I said thanks for dinner," I call over my shoulder as I walk out, slamming the door shut behind me.

Dad knows better than to come after me. Unfortunately for Detective Brennan, he doesn't.

"Piper!" He rushes down the driveway to my car, which I'm already getting into. "Wait." He grabs the door before I can close it.

"Let go." I start the engine and throw the gear into reverse. "I mean it, Detective. I will drive with you latched onto the door if necessary."

"You're seriously going to storm out of here instead of letting me help you?" He narrows his eyes at me, and I wonder if he's really seeing me or if he's seeing his mother.

"She was thirty thousand feet in the air. You couldn't have saved her even if she had asked for your help."

Stunned, he steps back, releasing my door. I grab the handle and slam the door shut, backing out before he can regain his composure and try to stop me.

I need to cool off, so I decide to drive around instead of heading home. I pull onto Route 209 and head south. As the scenery passes by my windows, my mind starts reeling. Victor said his daughter hated traffic and typically took back roads. That's why her car was found on Keystone instead of 209. But if someone did abduct her before she even left the house, they might have taken this road instead, brought Veronica somewhere, and then headed to Keystone to ditch the car. But then what? Was someone else waiting on Keystone to pick him up? There's nothing around there but woods and a small lake.

Boots. The person was wearing boots. Did that mean he was hiking to the place where he had Veronica? I reach up and rub my right temple, which is throbbing. A car honks behind me, its headlights blinding me in the rearview mirror. A quick glance at the speedometer tells me I'm doing thirty-five in a forty-five mile an hour zone. I pull over onto the shoulder and let the person pass me.

I take several deep breaths, hoping to clear my mind and see what I've been missing. Instead, my phone rings in my purse on the passenger seat. The Bluetooth connects, and I press the controls on the steering wheel.

"You don't know when to quit, do you?" I say.

"That was a low blow, Piper."

"Why do you insist that we're on a first-name basis, Detective?" I lean my head back on my seat.

"Maybe because, banter aside, I see you as an actual human being. It would be nice if you'd show me the same common courtesy."

"My head feels like it's splitting down the middle at the moment, so unless you're calling to tell me you're on your way with some aspirin, I wouldn't hold your breath waiting for me to show you some common courtesy."

"That explains why you were driving so far under the speed limit."

I jerk my head up and turn around in my seat. Brennan's Explorer is parked directly behind me, the lights off. "You tailed me?"

"What? You thought your little comment about my mom was enough to make me curl up in a ball on your parents' couch for the night?" He opens the driver's side door and steps out.

"You're infuriating."

"You only think that because I bested you." He walks toward my car, and I check to make sure the doors are still locked.

"You didn't best me by any means. Even dogs know how to follow."

"You're not a dog person? Is that why your parents insisted on gating Max at dinner tonight?" He reaches for my door handle and tugs. I smile when it doesn't open. He lowers his head and taps on the window with the knuckle of his pointer finger. "Are you seriously going to make me stand out here by myself?"

"I don't remember asking you to tag along in the first place."

He sighs into the phone and turns around, leaning his ass against my window. "Fine. We can talk like this if that's what you prefer."

"I'd prefer if you'd find the time to hit the gym. Your glutes are looking a little saggy in those pants."

He stands up straight and twists his head around to look at his backside. "They were pressed up against your window. Anyone—" He groans. "Whatever, Piper. Oh, I mean, Ms. Ashwell."

"Thank you. See, and you talk about me not being courteous. At least I address you properly."

"Yeah, well how about you tell me what you're doing out here. This isn't the way back to your apartment."

"How would you know?" He's never been to my place, and I've never told him where I live.

"I'm a detective, remember?"

"So what? You ran my name through the system?"

He shrugs, not even having the decency to appear the least bit guilty.

"You're unbelievable."

"You would've done the same with me."

"No, I wouldn't have, but I don't give a damn where you live, nor do I want to know anything else about you."

He leans down, peering through my window. "Because you already know everything you need to know about me, right? Or you *think* you do?"

I know I'm going to hate this as much as he will, but I lower my window and grab the arm holding his phone to his ear.

"What time should I pick you up tonight?" Brennan *reaches forward and twirls a lock of blonde hair around his finger.*

The woman giggles in response. "How about eight?"

He steps toward her. "Great. I'd love to see your place."

"Oh, let me give you directions."

"No need. I can run you through the system." *He takes another step, his foot falling between her black high-heels.* "Unless there's something on your record you don't want me to see."

She giggles again. "Depends. Would getting drunk and streaking down a crowded street on spring break show up on *my record?" The level of flirtation in her voice borders on whorish.*

"Maybe we could stay in and you could show me what that looked like."

I force myself to let go of Brennan's hand. The look of disgust on my face must be clear as day in the light of the streetlamp because he steps back and says, "What did you see?"

"Just how much of a pervert you really are." I raise my window again, and my hurried breaths quickly fog it. I forget our call is still connected and jump when his voice fills my car.

"What the hell did you see? You can't just do that to a person and then not tell them what you saw." I'm not sure if he's angry, worried, or embarrassed. "Damn it, Piper! Answer me!"

"I didn't see you naked, if that's what you're worried about. Believe me, I'd be clawing my eyes out if I did."

He tries the door again, but it's still locked. "Would you open the damn door?"

"Not a chance in hell. You're lucky I haven't hung up on your ass." I don't know why I want to know, but I ask, "Did you just meet that woman and you were going to go to her place and...?" I can't finish my statement.

"What woman?"

I turn to face him, but he's blurry through the fogged window. I lower it a few inches so I can see his eyes. "How many women do you jump into bed with the day you meet them?"

"I'm not sure how that's any of your business. You violated my privacy. You touched me with the intent of having a vision."

"You practically begged me to. You claim I don't know

you, but I do. That's why I'm keeping us off a first-name basis. We work together, Detective, but we'll never be friends." I put the car in gear and pull forward before turning back onto the road.

I curse myself for ever thinking Brennan and I could be friends. I can't have friends. I'm destined to be alone for life. I might not be clairvoyant, but I can see that much.

CHAPTER NINE

I'm at my office early Wednesday morning, downing a large toasted almond and shoveling a cranberry scone into my mouth. Google Earth is open on my laptop, allowing me to scan the woods near Keystone. If Veronica's abductor hiked somewhere after abandoning her car, there has to be some campsite or something in those woods. I find several south of Weltunkin in smaller towns along the Delaware River, but Weltunkin itself has become more populated and built-up over the years. Those back roads are only used by locals to avoid tourists.

My phone rings, and I glance at my iPhone to see Dad's face fill my display. I smile at the picture of him wearing a lobster bib. It was taken a year ago when we celebrated his birthday at his favorite seafood place in New Jersey.

"Took you long enough," I answer.

"Mitchell told me about your conversation last night. I figured you needed some time to cool off."

"He told you what I did?"

"That you reamed him out and left him standing on the side of the road? Yes."

So he didn't mention that I read him. Good. Dad would have more than a few choice words for me about that.

"He and I are heading to the Castells' now. Is there anything in specific you want me to look for? Anything I can maybe bring back for you to read?"

He's trying to help, but we both know he wouldn't steal anything from the Castells' garage and bring it back to me.

"Just do your thing, Dad. I'm sure you'll find something and you won't even need me." I zoom in on a patch of woods Google Earth just pulled up.

"You know I can't do this without you, Piper."

"Yeah, well it looks like you're going to have to. At least that part anyway."

"What are you working on? I hear you pressing keys on your laptop." From the sound of the car engine in the background, he and Brennan are already heading out to the Castells'.

"I pulled up directions to UPenn, and now I'm searching for campsites anywhere in the vicinity of Keystone."

"There aren't any. Don't waste your time. And why are you looking up directions to UPenn? Are you thinking of trying to find this Will person?"

"No." I zoom back out, the search not yielding anything useful. I push my laptop aside. "I'm trying to figure out if whoever took Veronica was actually heading back to the college. If it was this Will guy, then that's probably where he'd take her. It could be a fraternity prank: kidnap the girl who was supposed to dance at the rush party."

"I'm going to call the fraternities," Dad says. "I'll keep you posted." He hangs up without another word.

"This is ridiculous." I stand up, knowing what I need to do. I have to get to that garage and look around again. I have to find whatever it is that I'm missing. But how do I do that without the Castells knowing I'm there?

I grab my jacket and purse, figuring I'll come up with a plan on the way. Maybe trying to find a way to get into their house unseen will help me discover how Veronica's kidnapper did it. Think like a criminal and all that.

The first obstacle presents itself when I reach the bottom of their driveway. I can't exactly pull up behind Dad's car and act like I belong there. And if I leave my car at the bottom of the driveway and Mr. or Mrs. Castell happens to go out while I'm here, they'll see it for sure. I drive around, looking for a place to park that's not clearly visible. I passed a gas station about a quarter mile back, but then I'd run the risk of people seeing me. I keep heading north and come to a wooden gate. I stop in front of it, noticing it's not locked. All I can see are fields with a barn off in the distance. Do the Castells' have horses? Is this where they keep them boarded?

I open the gate, hurry back to my car, and drive through. The pathway is dirt and gravel, and rocks kick up, hitting the underside of my car. My Mazda wasn't built for off-roading, but I continue on, winding around a small hill and past the barn and stables. I park behind it, hoping my car will be out of view if anyone comes to take care of the horses while I'm here. I need to close the gate on my way up to the Castells' house before anyone drives by and sees it open, but something is pulling me toward the stables. I get out of the car and walk in the direction of the stables. There are four stalls in a line, and two heads and one ass are visible when I enter. The horse on the end, a gray palomino, whinnies when I pass by. The nameplate on the front of the stall reads *Sergeant Pepper*. I snicker to myself. The next one, belonging to a beautiful cream-colored horse, reads *Penny*

Lane. The third says *Maggie Mae*, and the last one is *Rocky Raccoon.* Definite Beatles fans. That's clear.

I step toward Maggie Mae's stall, but good old Maggie is the one with her rear end to me. I move to the last stall to get a better look at Rocky Raccoon, but the stall is empty. I peer inside, not sure what I'm expecting to see. Footprints? Some indication that Rocky is out being groomed or exercised?

My hand grips the edge of the stall.

"Bad boy, Rocky!" Veronica admonishes the black horse. "This is what I get for feeding you? You bite my hand?" She holds her hand, squeezing the palm where the teeth marks are denting her skin. "You're just lucky you didn't draw blood." She turns to Maggie Mae, the brown mare in the next stall. "Why can't you behave like Maggie here?" She reaches for Maggie's nose, petting it lovingly. "You're a good girl, aren't you, Maggie?"

A gloved hand flashes in front of Veronica's face as a white cloth is pressed to her nose and mouth.

This time, instead of the images fading away, I collapse on the stable floor.

———

"Miss? Miss, can you hear me?" someone says, tapping my cheek with a cold, calloused hand.

My eyes open slowly, my vision taking a moment to come into focus. A man in his late forties with graying hair and glasses looks down at me. "Who are you?" I ask, my voice groggy.

"I was about to ask you the same thing." He helps me to a sitting position, my back against Rocky's stall.

"My name is Piper Ashwell. I'm a private investigator working on the Castell case." Even though I'm not technically supposed to be here, I figure my title and connection to the case is the best way to go.

"I see. Can I ask what you're doing down here?"

"Where's Rocky?" I gesture behind me to the empty stall.

"Rocky has been known to get loose. I discovered his empty stall on Sunday when I came to tend to the horses." He sighs. "I was hoping to get him back before Mrs. Castell found out. She loves these horses and blames me every time Rocky gets out."

"Are they her horses?" I ask, getting to my feet since the concrete slab I'm sitting on is freezing my ass through my jeans.

"No. They're Veronica's. Though Veronica never liked Rocky very much. He's a biter."

I look down at my hand, the same hand that felt the piercing of Rocky's teeth when he bit Veronica in my vision. "She preferred Maggie, right?"

The man cocks his head at me. "How'd you know?"

"Private investigator, remember? It's my job to know things like this." I look him up and down now that I'm feeling like myself again. "What did you say your name was?" I ask, knowing he never offered his name.

He wipes his hand on the front of his jeans. "Where are my manners?" He extends his right hand to me. "I'm Terrance Walsh, but you can call me Terry."

"Nice to meet you, Terry," I say, shaking his hand. I motion to the empty stall. "Does Rocky usually take off for long periods of time?"

Terry turns and looks out over the open fields. "Not like this. He usually comes home when he gets hungry. The dang horse only eats special order food. He's spoiled rotten if you ask me. Mr. Castell pays a fortune to keep his daughter's horses happy and in prime showing condition."

I nod, not that I care about any of that. Though Rocky's disappearance does coincide with Veronica's. "You said you didn't notify the Castells that Rocky is missing."

"No, I didn't. Like I said, I was hoping he'd come back by now. I didn't want to bother them, what with Miss Veronica being missing." He lets out a deep breath. "Doesn't look like I have a choice, though."

Or maybe he doesn't want to mention Rocky's disappearance because he used Rocky to bring him wherever he was going after he ditched Veronica's car. A horse could travel farther in a shorter amount of time than a person on foot. I need to read him. I look around, noticing a horseshoe on the ground a few feet away. I move toward it, keeping my eyes locked on Terry so he doesn't suspect anything. "If you'd like, I could drive around the grounds and help you search for—" I step on the horseshoe and pretend to turn my ankle. With a small cry of pain, I allow myself to fall onto the grass in front of the stable.

"Are you all right, Ms. Ashwell?" Terry rushes over to help me up.

I latch onto his hand and clear all thoughts from my mind.

"Please, Terry," Veronica pleads. "You can't tell them. Daddy would kill me if he found out."

Terry puts his hands up in front of him. "Miss Veronica, this isn't any of my business."

Veronica nods. "That's right. It's not." She thrusts a pregnancy test at him. "So take this out with the rest of the trash, and don't say a word about it to anyone."

Terry looks down at the test, which has a negative reading. "Why are you worried if you aren't pregnant anyway?"

Veronica lowers her head. "You know my father. Can you imagine what he'd do if he found out I had to take one of these? Mom put me on birth control at fourteen. I'm the stupid idiot who left my pills here when school started. I never should've..." She raises her eyes. "Why am I telling you this?"

"I don't want to know any of it. It's none of my business who you're..." He motions to the pregnancy test.

Veronica scoffs. "God, you're just like Daddy. You probably think I'm off at school whoring around, don't you?" She shakes her head. "Everyone thinks I'm the little rich girl rebelling because she doesn't have a care in the world and doesn't know what to do with herself. 'Dance for all our rushees, Veronica. Put those dance lessons your daddy paid for to good use.' God, do you have any idea how degrading that is? Will can go fuck himself. Him and his frat buddies. I got drunk at one party and hooked up with him, and now he thinks he's my fucking pimp. 'Do this or I'll show everyone the video I made of you. Pay my rent or I'll show the video.' Him and his damn video. He drugged me! He drugged me and then pretended he loved me to get away with it. Well, I'm done. I'm done with him, and I'm done with that school. I'm never going back there! Never! I'd rather run away and spend my life with Rocky, who'd probably eat me in my sleep, before I let Will and Theta Chi ruin my reputation.

"I think maybe we should get you to a doctor," Terry says, helping me to my feet once I come to.

"No. I'm fine. Really." Better than fine. I know which Will we're looking for. He's a member of Theta Chi. "I have to go. I hope you find Rocky, Terry." I rush around the stables to my car and hop inside, dialing Dad's cell. He answers as I'm turning onto the path that leads back to the road.

"Piper, we're just finishing up."

"I am, too. I know who we're looking for, and I'm not so sure Veronica was really kidnapped either."

"What are you talking about?" Detective Brennan says, and I realize Dad must have his phone on speaker.

"Where are you two?" I ask.

"In the car, heading back to the station. Where are you?"

I smile to myself as I pull onto the road. "Leaving the Castells' stables."

"They have horses?" Dad asks.

"And one's missing." I fill them in on what I found out.

"So she was sleeping with that Will guy and thought she was pregnant?" Brennan huffs. "Why would she continue to sleep with him if he was blackmailing her and making her do all that stuff for him?"

"She thought he loved her. In both of my visions that mentioned Will, I sensed this strange tension in their relationship. She clearly wanted to believe he cared about her, but both times the conversations ended heatedly, with her being angry at Will because of the things he wanted her to do."

"That's seriously messed up," Brennan says.

"For once I agree with you."

"We need to talk to Will," Dad interrupts. "ASAP."

"I agree. Though if the horse is involved, I doubt Will is actually at UPenn."

"Let me make a few calls. I'll see if I can get a hold of him through the fraternity," Dad says. "Meet us at the station."

"Will do." I hang up and smile the whole way to the police station. We have our first real lead.

CHAPTER TEN

The station is pretty quiet when I walk in. I know just about everyone here thanks to Dad, but I don't like coming into the station. It's always filled with emotions running on high. The atmosphere is overwhelming to someone like me. Still, I need to talk to Dad and Detective Brennan, and Dad's best resources are here.

"There she is," Detective Brennan says as I approach Dad's desk. He's sitting in the seat opposite Dad, and he stands when I get there, pulling a chair from a nearby desk so we can all sit together.

"Okay," I dive right in as I sit. "Someone used chloroform to knock Veronica out while she was at the stables on Saturday evening."

"You didn't see who?" Detective Brennan asks.

I shake my head. "Only a leather driving glove. She was attacked from behind. I smelled the chloroform, though."

"Where would a college student get chloroform?" Dad asks. "If it was in fact this Will character."

"Are you kidding?" Brennan says. "There are YouTube videos on how to make the stuff with bleach and acetone."

"Why do you know that?" My mind flashes with images of the woman I saw in my vision the other night. I quickly dismiss it, though. Brennan would never do something like that. With his looks, he probably has no trouble getting women to do whatever he asks. No help needed from the sweet-smelling compound.

"The question is who used chloroform on Veronica to knock her out," Brennan answers, ignoring my inquiry.

I lower my gaze, wishing I had never said it. "Will is the likely suspect, but he'd been at UPenn when he called her Friday night. It's possible he drove the three hours to be here the next day, though. If he was angry enough, he'd do it. Showing that video would mean losing his leverage over her. He wouldn't play that card yet. At least I don't think he would. So maybe he tried to scare her."

"You mean he knocked her out to prove what he could do to her if she didn't cooperate with him?" Brennan cringes. "Please tell me I get to interrogate this asshole." His hands clench and unclench repeatedly.

"Speaking of Will..." Dad turns his laptop so we can see his screen. "His name is William Catton. He's a junior at UPenn and vice president of the Theta Chi chapter there. The entire chapter was on probation three years ago after a possible hazing incident."

"Will would have been a freshman at the time," I say. "Think this is payback of some sort?"

"Why would he take it out on Veronica?" Brennan asks. "She was in high school at the time."

"And from what you said, Will was throwing a party for the rushees," Dad adds, clasping his hands in front of him on his desk. "Maybe he's throwing the parties in an attempt to make sure the rushees don't complain about hazing. As vice president of the fraternity, he'd be one of the individuals held responsible if hazing charges did come up."

"Okay, so he's using Veronica to help him save face for the fraternity. But why? Why her? What's their connection?" I check out the rest of the information about Will Catton. "He's from Newark, New Jersey."

"There's a place no one ever visits."

"Unless you need a flight," I say.

"It's a rough neighborhood, though," Brennan continues. "So the kid is no stranger to crimes, most likely."

"He got into UPenn, so he's either wicked smart or his parents have a lot of money to donate to the school." I keep scanning the information on Catton. "It's not money. His mom died of cancer when he was six. His dad is a janitor in a local school. Catton got into UPenn on an academic scholarship." I lean back in the chair and take a deep breath. This kid clearly has the brains to pull off a kidnapping like this. I study his picture, hoping it will bring some sort of vision to light, but pictures don't usually help me. Not unless the person actually touched the picture.

"Anything?" Dad asks, knowing what I'm trying and failing to do.

I shake my head. "I can't even tell much about him from the picture." His hair is sandy brown and cut short. He has it spiky in the front, which is a trend I'd love to see go away and never return. His eyes are pale blue, and he has a clef chin. I guess if I were a college-age girl I'd find him mildly attractive. Though I suspect Veronica's fascination with him has more to do with her saving face for her drunken—and drugged—indiscretions than any real feelings for Will.

"Road trip?" Brennan asks.

"As it turns out," Dad says, "Will left campus sometime Saturday and hasn't returned."

"No!" I say. "That's almost too easy. Will is smart. If he did something to Veronica, he'd make sure he was back in time to attend at least a few classes so no one got suspicious."

"Maybe he's not as bright as you think he is," Detective Brennan says with a shrug. "Or maybe he thought he could handle this and got in way over his head. He could be panicking and making it up as he goes now."

"Dad, who did you talk to at UPenn to find out Will hasn't been back?"

"His roommate. A guy named"—Dad flips through the legal pad on his desk—"Jakai Jackson. They share an off-campus house that acts as a fraternity house even though they don't officially call it that."

"Did you record the call?" Brennan asks.

Dad nods. "Of course, but there's not much to it. Just Jakai telling me he hasn't seen Will since Saturday. He said Will sometimes goes home for a few days to visit and didn't think it was a big deal."

Except a girl is missing and might even be dead by now. "We need to find him. Now."

"Why are you so worried all of a sudden?" Brennan cocks his head at me, and I don't like the way his eyes seem to stare through me.

"I don't know. But there's been no ransom note. Why? If this was about money, there would be some communication from the kidnapper."

"Unless the person who kidnapped Veronica wants her to withdraw her own money from her bank account. Did we freeze those?" Detective Brennan asks Dad.

"Victor Castell already did. He froze all of their accounts in fear that money was the cause of all this."

"For a man who seems to love his daughter so much,

he's taking every precaution to secure his money." I narrow my eyes. "What if he does get a ransom note? How does he intend to bargain with the kidnapper?"

"He doesn't." Dad's face loses all color. "He told me he won't entertain discussions about money. He might love his daughter, but the man loves his lifestyle more."

I leave the police station and head to my office, not sure what to make of any of this. Dad and Brennan are working to track down William Catton so we can hopefully find him and interrogate him. In the meantime, I'm trying to figure out how I misread Victor Castell. Right from the start, this case has been so difficult. Normally, I read a few personal belongings and find the victim. Case closed. This time, even when I think my visions make sense, they throw me for a loop.

Where the hell are all of Veronica's belongings? Why aren't they at her house or in her car? Unless...

I dial Detective Brennan, assuming he's sitting there while Dad is busy doing the actual police work.

"What's up, Piper?" he answers on the second ring.

"What if Veronica was planning to run away before she was kidnapped? That would explain why we couldn't find any of her things in her car. She seemed afraid to go back to school and afraid to disappoint her parents by telling them what was really going on. She could have taken the horse and split. Terry said the horse took off a lot, but what if it wasn't doing it on its own. What if Veronica was taking it somewhere to dump her stuff little by little so no one would notice?"

"Whoa, slow down, and repeat that for your dad. I'm putting you on speaker."

I wait while Brennan switches to speaker and then repeat my theory.

"Okay, that makes sense," Dad says once I'm finished. "The Castells have a few other places, but they're all too far to travel on horse."

"She wouldn't go where her parents could find her. She was trying to get away from them, too. I think they put on a good show, but they're not the happy, loving family they want us all to think they are. They're even fooling each other." As soon as I say it, I know it's true. It's an act. Victor Castell is pretending to be distraught over his daughter's disappearance because that's what the public would want him to do. Mrs. Castell might be objecting to my involvement in the case for the same reason. Because the overprotective, loving mother wouldn't put her daughter's life in the hands of a woman who claims to have visions.

"Piper, did we lose you?" Dad asks.

"No, sorry." I park my car, switch the phone off Bluetooth, and get out.

"You shouldn't drive when you're deep in thought like that," Dad says. "You know what can happen."

Yes, I know. I could have a vision and wind up in a ditch or even killing someone. I shouldn't do most things normal people do all the time. I'm sick of hearing it, though. I wave to Marcia, who is putting the closed sign on the door of her store.

"See you in the morning," she calls to me.

I nod and open the door to my office. "I think we're dealing with a family who is great at cover-ups."

"You think they're all in on it together? Like maybe Veronica wasn't kidnapped to begin with?" Detective Brennan asks.

"That would be different, but no. She was kidnapped all right. Her parents just don't care as much as they're letting on. Think about it. Veronica attends an Ivy League school, but have you seen her grades?" I looked them up this morning. "They're less than Ivy League material. Her father bought her way into that school, and she's throwing his money away. Sure, she got drunk and possibly drugged by Will at a fraternity party, and now he's blackmailing her. He's a dick for that. But do we really believe that was the only time she's done something crazy? The only time she partied that hard? Will said she's a great dancer, and the way he said it implied she'd danced for his frat before. And I'm not talking about ballet."

"Damn, I went to college about two decades too early," Detective Brennan says.

"Dad, please smack him upside the head for me." I scoff in disgust. "Hasn't anyone taught you to have an internal filter?"

"Like you've never been to a strip club?" He immediately shuts up, so I can imagine the look Dad gave him.

"No, I haven't. And that internal filter would have been great twenty seconds ago before you made a comment like that in front of my father, you ass."

"Enough! The both of you. I swear you bicker like brother and sister." He's quiet for a moment, and I wait for the lecture I know is coming. "Piper, I can't ground you anymore, but I can remove you from a case. And, Mitchell, I can request a partner change, so I suggest you two get over whatever the hell you call this feud you have going before you're both out of jobs."

"Sorry," Brennan and I both mutter.

"Now, I'm going to track down Catton. Piper, I want you and Brennan to go back to those stables and stay there until you have concrete evidence for me. If that's where Veronica was kidnapped, you should be able to get more than just chloroform and a glove from your visions. Brennan will pick you up in five." He hangs up.

God, that man still instills fear in me with the mere tone of his voice.

I lock up and wait outside for Detective Brennan, leaning against the trunk of my Mazda. I'm starving, not having stopped to eat since my scone this morning. One thing about this job, it's like constantly being on a diet.

The black Explorer pulls up in the empty spot next to me, and the passenger window opens. "If you're waiting for me to get out and open the door for you, you're going to freeze your ass off. It's getting cold." He pretends to shiver for effect.

I open the door and get inside. "Then put the windows up, genius."

He backs out of the spot before I can even get my door shut. "Jeez!" I slam the door and click my seat belt into place. Before I can yell, I smell pepperoni. I turn to find a hot pizza on the back seat. "Don't mind if I do." I open the box, seeing four slices missing.

"Sure, go ahead and eat my food. I don't mind at all. Feel free to drink the rest of my Coke here as well." He picks up the Styrofoam cup and gives it a shake, the ice sloshing back and forth.

"Put my lips anywhere your mouth was? No thank you." I take a bite of pizza.

"How do you know I didn't lick that slice?" He raises a questioning brow at me.

"Because no one licks pizza, not even a pig like you." I take another bite and then another until my mouth can barely close while I chew.

"Attractive," he says with a shake of his head.

"I'm not trying to impress you," I say around the food in my mouth.

"Good thing."

We drive the rest of the way in silence, and I eat another slice of pizza. When I'm finished, I look around for a napkin.

"In the glove compartment."

Glove compartment. Gloves! "That's it!"

"Yes, that's the glove compartment. Very good, hotshot private investigator." He rolls his eyes, and I smack his arm with my greasy fingers.

"No! My vision. I kept seeing gloves. I think I was supposed to check the glove compartment."

"Your visions are that cryptic? Why not just see the glove compartment?"

I grab a napkin and wipe my hands. "Why not just see the location of the missing person?" I counter.

"Fine. I see your point. But what do you think we'll find in the glove compartment?"

"I have no idea. Maybe the pocketknife used to slash the tire. If so, I could read it and know for sure who it belongs to."

"That would help. It would give us concrete evidence and possibly fingerprints, too."

We're getting close to the Castells' house, and I motion for him to keep going.

"The stables are up further on the left. And you'd only get fingerprints if the kidnapper used the knife before he put on the gloves."

"He? I think that's the first time I've heard you mention the gender of the kidnapper."

"Turn here!" I say, jerking the steering wheel.

"Damn it! Would you stop doing that?" Brennan slams

on the brakes before taking out the wooden gate, which is clearly locked now.

"Park here. We're going to have to go on foot." I unclick my seat belt and hop out. Brennan follows my lead, though he's not fazed by the chilly night air, whereas I tug my jacket more tightly around my body.

"If you had an ounce of fat on you, you wouldn't be so cold."

I turn and glare at him. "It's genetic. My metabolism works at hyper speed."

"Neither of your parents is as thin as you." He stops at the gate as I climb up and over it. I notice he puts his hands out, ready to catch me should I fall.

I drop down on the other side. "I take after my grandmother on my mom's side. Apparently, it skipped a generation."

Brennan hops the gate with ease, landing next to me. "Lucky you."

I'm not sure how to take the comment, so I steer the conversation back to the case. "You were right before. I don't think I have mentioned the gender of the kidnapper before now. I'm not sure who it actually is, but I feel like it's a male."

"You *feel*? Like a gut feeling? Or is it because you suspect Will Catton?" He eyes me, which makes me look everywhere but in his direction. I start down the path, and he keeps in step with me.

"Neither, actually. I just know some things. They pop into my mind as facts. It's sort of like a vision but with no visual aid."

"I think I understand." He gets quiet for a moment. "Do you think...? No, never mind."

I stop and turn to him, placing my hand on his arm. I'm hoping he doesn't know why until it's too late.

"We've been through this. Mommy has to go away for a few days."

"Can't I come, too?" Mitchell clutches his mother's hand.

"No, Mitchell. You have to stay here and take care of things for me." She looks around at their living room.

"But Dad can do that."

"Not like you can." She bends down, leaning her head on top of his. *"You are my little man. And I want you to remember that even though you're young, you are capable of doing great things. I know you'll make a difference in people's lives. You're meant to."* She kisses the top of his head. *"We're all meant for different things. We can't change that."* Her eyes fill with tears. *"I have to go now, sweetheart."*

When the vision fades, I'm left with this overwhelming feeling of sorrow. Brennan's mother had this empty pit in her stomach when she spoke to Mitchell. She wasn't scared. She was heartbroken. She knew she was going to die, and she got on that plane anyway. Why? She could have taken a different flight. Instead, she chose to die.

CHAPTER ELEVEN

"You know, don't you?" Brennan turns away from me and walks further down the path toward the barn. "You did that on purpose in order to find out."

I'm still rooted in the same spot, not sure if he's angry, upset, or looking for a shoulder to cry on. "Mitchell." The sound of his first name coming off my lips makes him stop walking and turn back to me.

"What's that? Pity? Pity for the kid whose mom willingly chose to get on that plane she knew would crash?" His voice hitches at the end, and he places a hand over his eyes, his thumb and forefinger each pressed to a temple.

"You suspected, didn't you?" I ask, slowly moving toward him.

He nods but doesn't lower his hand. "I thought she was happy. That she loved my brother and me."

I want to ask about his father, but I decide it's best not to. Instead, I focus on what I know to be true. "She was sure she was meant to die that day. I got the impression your mother believed in fate or some greater plan. She accepted what she saw as absolute." I reach my hand out, gently grasping the elbow of his bent arm, which is still shielding his eyes from me. "She didn't want to die. She simply believed she had to."

Mitchell jerks his arm away, revealing bloodshot eyes. He manages to hold back his tears as he yells, "That's bull-shit! If she didn't get on that plane, she'd still be here. I wouldn't have had to grow up without a mother. With only a father who—" He looks away, staring off into the distance. "Did you see that, too? Do you want to take my hand and find out all my secrets?"

"I'm sorry. I shouldn't have tried to get a read off you." He'd already made it clear he didn't want me touching him, yet I went ahead and did it anyway. "I promise I won't do it again." I hold my hands up to emphasize the point.

He runs a shaky hand through his hair. "He hired a nanny so he wouldn't have to look at my brother and me. Said we looked too much like Mom and it was too painful to see our faces. We spent holidays with the nanny's family while Dad stayed home and buried his sorrows at the bottom of a bottle of bourbon."

"You don't have to tell me."

"You wanted to know, right? You pried, so I'm telling." He holds his arms out to the sides. "You want to know why I'm such a dick most of the time? It's genetic. Nick takes after our mom. Me, I'm apparently like Dad."

I step toward him but think twice about it. No physical contact. "You're not. You're out here helping people every day. From what you've said, that's nothing like your father."

He runs his tongue across his front teeth as he considers what I said. "Maybe you're right. Or maybe I chose this job as a pathetic attempt to be different than him." His eyes meet mine for the first time since I had the vision. "He never remarried, but boy did he have his share of women.

Treated them terribly, and I never understood why they'd all agree to go out with him." His voice softens. "Until now."

Because he treats women just as terribly and is never at a loss for a date when he wants one. I don't verbalize that, knowing he's already well aware.

"I have a proposal for you."

He laughs. "I admit to being a womanizer and you're going to propose?"

I roll my eyes, but I let him have his little joke given I'm the one who sent him into this depression. "I'm proposing we call a truce. You were right all along. We work together and should call each other by our first names."

"I've been calling you Piper from day one."

"Yeah, but that was to piss me off. I'm giving you permission now."

He smirks. "Way to take all the fun out of it." He nudges my arm with his elbow to show he's only teasing.

"Watch it now. You just made physical contact with me."

He looks down at my forearm where he touched me. "Does it work that easily?"

I shake my head. "You're safe."

"So, let me get this straight. You're not going to call me *Detective* anymore? You're going to call me Mitchell?"

I take a few steps in the direction of the barn. "Actually, I was thinking of giving you a nickname. Something along the lines of *Mitchy-poo*. Unless you're getting on my nerves. Then I'm calling you *Bitch*." I look over my shoulder at him, and he follows me. "See what I did there? Mitch...Bitch?"

"Yeah, I got it. You're a freakin' cutup."

I give a small curtsy and keep walking toward the barn and stables. As I approach, my heart nearly stops. All four stables are occupied. "What?" I run the rest of the way.

"This can't be." I rush over to Rocky's stable, and the black horse neighs in protest when I get too close. At the last second, I remember he's a biter and I step back.

"The horse is back," Mitchell says.

"Thank you, Captain Obvious."

"I see calling me Mitchell is over before it even began." He checks the other stalls, confirming they're all occupied.

"This is serious. My entire theory was based on this horse being gone." I peer into Rocky's big brown eyes. "Were you really just out for a stroll on your own?"

"Why not read him and find out?" Mitchell asks, stepping up beside me and reaching for Rocky's snout.

I swat his hand away. "Careful. He's a biter. I saw—and felt—him bite Veronica."

"Sucks to be you, then, since you have to touch him."

It's too late to call Terry to find out what actually happened or to get a muzzle for Rocky. "Think you can get him to turn around?"

"Trying to grope a horse's ass now?" Mitchell cocks a brow at me.

"More like trying to keep my hand."

"You have two." He holds both hands up in front of him, doing a pretty darn impressive display of jazz hands.

"Former cheerleader?" I ask, pointing to his waggling fingers.

He turns both middle fingers upward, folding the others back. "Funny."

"The truth is, I only read objects with my right hand."

His eyes narrow on me. "So you can touch things and people with your left hand and nothing happens?"

"You're a quick study."

"Meaning, if you lost your right hand somehow, you'd also lose your job?"

I have a degree in criminal justice and a PI license, but I get what he's saying. "Are you going to help me with this horse or not?" I ask, directing his attention back to more important things.

"How do you expect me to turn the horse around? Besides, do you really want to be on that end of him?" He stands on his toes to get a better look at Rocky's backside. "Maybe I can feed him so his mouth is busy eating instead of trying to take a bite out of you."

A feedbag could work. I raise a finger and head inside the barn, searching for a feedbag. Mitchell follows behind me, and for once he doesn't fill the silence with the sound of his voice. I look around at the bales of hay, horse brushes, hoses, and bags of feed. "Perfect." I go to the food and scoop some into the feedbag next to it, giving Mitchell a smile in the process.

He takes it from me. "Let me." He must not want to risk me not having my hand to evoke visions because he's willing to get bit for me. I watch him as he brings the feedbag over to Rocky. "Hey, boy. You hungry?" He lets Rocky sniff the food before he secures the bag over the horse's head. "Got it." He steps back with a satisfied smile. "You're up."

"Great. Now let's find out what good old Rocky knows." I reach my hand for the top of Rocky's head, which isn't easy to see in the increasing darkness of the night. I feel the velvety soft fur between his eyes and continue reaching higher so I don't accidentally poke the horse in the eye and make him angry if the vision gets too intense. Finding his mane, I settle my hand there and take several deep breaths.

"Stupid bitch. You thought you could tell me how it was going to be. I don't think so. I own you." William Catton stands over Veronica's limp body, lying in a heap on the cold cement in front of the stables.

Rocky whinnies and kicks at the stable door.

"What's your problem?" Will asks, lashing out at the horse. "You want out?" Will looks back and forth between the horse and Veronica. "Maybe that's not a bad idea. I could make it look like Veronica took you for a ride. That would buy me some time."

Will unhooks the latch on the stable door and steps back. Rocky takes a few tentative steps out of the stall, his hooves dangerously close to Veronica's head on the ground. Will waves the white cloth in his hand at the horse's face. "Go on! Get out of here!"

Rocky snaps his teeth at Will, trying to take a bite at either him or the cloth. Will retaliates by swinging a fist at the horse. Rocky rears up, kicking his legs and knocking Will to the ground. As Rocky's hooves come back down, one connects with Veronica's head. Then Rocky takes off, running away through the open fields.

I come to in Mitchell's arms. He's cradling me in his lap on the ground. My eyelids flutter open, and I feel like my skull is cracked down the middle.

"Piper? Are you okay? Can you hear me?" Mitchell pushes my hair out of my face, and the contact with my head makes me wince.

"Don't touch," I manage to say.

"I don't care about giving you a vision. I need to make sure you're okay."

"No," I say. "My head."

Realization dawns on him. "Do you need a doctor?"

My injury isn't physical. I only feel the pain of Veronica's wound. Rocky gave her a concussion at the very least. "It's not real," I force out. "It will pass." Only it might take time.

Mitchell scoops me up and carries me back up the path

to his Explorer. Normally I'd protest, but I don't think I could stand on my own right now. Did Veronica wake up after being assaulted with chloroform and a horse hoof? Is she even still alive? Or am I searching for her body at this point? If she's dead, it would explain why there hasn't been a ransom note.

I try to still my thoughts as Mitchell puts me in the passenger seat and then takes his seat behind the wheel. I keep my eyes closed to block out all light as he drives. A few minutes later, he parks the car and comes around to help me out. I'm still having trouble focusing, but I know the two-story condo in front of me isn't mine.

"Where are we?" I ask, clutching my head like it will break in two if I don't hold it together.

"My place." He scoops me up again and carries me to the front door. He's almost too good at unlocking the door and bringing me inside, making me wonder how many women he's carried across this threshold.

He brings me into a living room and places me on the couch. He turns on a lamp on the table next to me, but I cringe.

"No lights. Please." My eyes can't take the brightness.

"Sorry." He clicks it off. "Let's try to sit you up. I'm not sure you should fall asleep. At least not until I know what kind of injury you're dealing with."

"Concussion," I say, keeping my voice a whisper in the hopes that he'll follow suit.

"Has this happened before?" His tone is softer, thankfully. "Do you feel the same effects of the victim often?"

I try to nod, but it hurts too much.

"Let me get you some aspirin and water. I'll be right back." He gets up slowly as if trying to judge whether I'll be okay on my own for a minute. I raise one hand and wave him away. He backs out of the room, keeping an eye on me until he's forced to turn the corner.

I lean my head back on the couch, willing this feeling to pass. *It's not real,* I mentally chant. But it is. The pain at least. Poor Veronica. But at least now I know William Catton is our guy. Enraged that she wouldn't submit to his demands, he drove to Weltunkin, knocked Veronica out with chloroform, and then tried to make it look like Veronica took off on one of her horses. Now the question I need to answer is where did he actually take her since it wasn't back to UPenn? And more importantly is she still alive?

CHAPTER TWELVE

I wake up Thursday morning to the sunlight shining in the window. I immediately shield my eyes, noticing my head is still throbbing from the aftereffects of the monster headache my vision incited last night. It takes me exactly thirty seconds to remember I'm at Mitchell's house. I sit up, taking in the barely furnished condo. A couch and one chair face a large screen TV mounted above the stone fireplace. The coffee table in front of me is full of watermarks left by many cold drinks.

"Hey," Mitchell says, walking in with two cups of steaming coffee. "I thought I heard you up." He hands me a mug with a Playboy bunny emblem on the front.

"Classy," I say, my voice thick from sleep, before taking a sip.

"The mugs were a gift from my brother. He meant it as a joke." Mitchell bobs a shoulder. "I gave him a pair of dice to hang from his rearview mirror. We've always given each other gag gifts."

"Avoiding feelings or just bad shoppers?" I ask, indulging in another sip of the French roast.

"A little of both most likely." He sits down on the couch next to me. "You sleep okay?"

"Yeah. Thanks for letting me crash here."

"What was I supposed to do? You literally fell into my arms after that vision. I wasn't dropping you off at home to get better on your own."

"You could have brought me to my parents' house." By the look of astonishment on his face it's clear the thought hadn't crossed his mind.

"That probably would have been the smart thing to do. I bet your dad is used to handling this sort of thing. You said it's happened before."

I clasp my coffee cup in both hands and bring my legs up on the couch. "Yeah. I hate to make him worry though, so it's good you didn't take me there."

"Look, I know I'm not your favorite person, but if I'm being completely honest, neither of us has many friends."

I laugh. "Truer words might never have been spoken."

"You've seen me at some of my most vulnerable times." His voice lowers, and he stares into his coffee. "I dare say you might know the real me better than anyone after that."

"Are you asking me to be your friend?" Yesterday, I would have made fun of him for this, but he did just take care of me and I can't help seeing his logic.

"I kind of think I am." He looks up at me. "I feel like I'm back in middle school."

"Uh-uh. In middle school, boys still think girls have cooties." I sip my coffee again.

"You mean you don't?" he asks with a smirk.

"Possibly, but I think you're equally likely to have cooties, so we should be fine." I hold up my right hand. "Besides, I'm a 'hands to myself' kind of person thanks to my gifts."

His head dips toward his right shoulder. "That's the first time you've referred to your abilities as gifts. I didn't think you saw them that way at all."

"Because most days I don't." I turn and look at the window behind the couch. "But thanks to them, I'm going to find Veronica Castell."

Before Mitchell can respond, his cell rings. He holds up a finger and pulls the phone from his back pocket. "It's your dad," he tells me before answering the call, putting it on speaker so I can hear. "What's the word, partner?"

"Mitchell, I need you and Piper to get down to the station right away."

"What's going on?" I ask, speaking loudly and leaning forward so he can hear me clearly.

"Piper? Where are you two?"

I'm tempted to say my office to avoid having to tell him about me spending the night on his partner's couch. Dad wants Mitchell and me to get along better, but I don't think a sleepover is what he had in mind.

"We're at my condo, sir."

Sir? I narrow my eyes at Mitchell, who just shrugs and mouths, "I panicked."

I stifle a laugh, knowing he's worried my father will jump to the wrong conclusion. "We've been up all night discussing the case. I had another vision, and I think it's going to help us find Veronica," I say.

Mitchell's eyes widen at my white lie, and I shrug and mouth, "I panicked," which makes him smile.

"Okay, well get down here. Victor Castell brought me a ransom note this morning."

———

Fifteen minutes later, Mitchell and I storm into the police station and straight to Dad's desk. He's hunched over a paper in front of him.

"Let me see it," I say, thrusting my hand out, knowing this is where I come in. I can read the note in a way neither he nor Mitchell can.

Mitchell reaches for my forearm, gripping it gently. "Wait."

I turn to glare at him. "What are you doing? This is how I'm going to find her. This is the clue I've been needing." I'm sure of it.

"Are you sure you're ready to do this?" His gaze shifts to about three inches above mine. "Your head."

Dad looks back and forth between us. "What exactly happened last night?"

"We went back to the stables. Rocky, Veronica's horse, isn't missing anymore. I read him and discovered William Catton is the one who used the chloroform on Veronica. He was pissed that she didn't go back to UPenn when he told her to, so he came to get her himself. Then he got the brilliant idea to release Rocky to make it look like Veronica took off for a joy ride on the horse. He said it would buy him time. I'm not sure what that meant, but the horse lashed out, kicked Will, and ended up connecting with Veronica's head afterward."

Mitchell listens just as intently as Dad since this is the first I've been able to discuss my last vision. "So he's definitely the kidnapper. We need to put out an APB on William Catton."

Dad nods. "Okay, this is good. Now we just need to find out where he's keeping Veronica." Dad slides the ransom note across the desk to me.

I take a seat, ready to find this creep and put him behind

bars. William Catton is a pervert and a sick bastard. It's going to give me great joy to lock the guy up. My eyes take in the ransom note first. It's on plain white computer paper. And it's typed, which means Catton was smart enough not to let his handwriting out him. I hold my right hand, palm flat, above the paper.

Dad gives me an encouraging nod, and I lower my hand.

It's dark. Foggy. Wet. Trees drip with rain. Dampness clings to my forehead. Veronica's forehead. Her head lolls to the side, pounding like her skull has been cracked open. Cold mud splatters against her left cheek just below her eye. She flinches, which makes her head hurt more. The searing pain nearly shatters my head in two.

I cry out, slamming my open palm against my forehead. "The woods. She's in the woods." I can't manage to get any more words out. The sounds in the police station are reverberating through my head like strikes to a gong. I can't take it. It's too much. The pain is blinding. My vision goes black.

———

When I wake up, I'm lying in a hospital bed with wires hooked up to me. "What the hell?" I start tugging at them, which makes the machine next to me beep like crazy.

A nurse rushes in. "Don't do that. Ms. Ashwell, please calm down." She pushes me back down by my shoulders, trying to restrain me.

"Let go of me. I'm fine. I need to get out of here." I need to get my hands back on that ransom note. My vision wasn't finished. I need to see more. Feel more. The police will never find Veronica if they have to search all the woods between here and UPenn.

"Doctor!" the nurse yells.

"Would you please get off of me?" I struggle against her, but she easily has me by about forty pounds.

"Doctor!" she yells again.

With my hands locked on her arms, I know what she intends to do. It's as clear as day in my mind. She wants to sedate me. I won't let her.

I steady my voice even though I want to scream. "Nurse?"

She yells for the doctor one more time before turning to see my face. "What?"

"I'm sorry. I'm okay now. I just woke up and didn't know where I was. You can let go. I understand you're trying to help me, and I won't try to pull these wires off." I keep eye contact, hoping she'll believe me.

Slowly, she releases her grip.

A doctor comes hurrying through the doorway. "What's going on?"

"I'm sorry," I say. "I was scared. I don't know why I'm here. I didn't mean to freak out."

He and the nurse exchange a look. "Since I'm here, let me check your vitals."

"Can I ask who brought me here?"

"Your father," the doctor says, reading the numbers off the machine next to my bed.

"Is he still here?"

The doctor shakes his head. There is a man in the waiting room, though. He said to notify him when you woke up.

"Mitchell?" I ask even though I know it couldn't be anyone else.

The doctor narrows his eyes. "I don't recall his name at the moment."

"Would you send him in, please?" Playing nice is

exhausting. I want to throw the covers off me and storm out of here, but I know that will only make the doctor whip out a needle and follow through with the nurse's plan to sedate me. "Please," I add, "it would make me feel better to see a familiar face."

Satisfied I'm not about to flee or flat line, the doctor nods and exits the room. The nurse stands at the foot of my bed with her arms crossed. Apparently, she's not as easily convinced.

"Piper?" Mitchell says, coming into the room. He walks past the nurse and stands next to my bed.

I look in the nurse's direction and then back at Mitchell.

"Could you give us a minute, please?" he asks her, flashing his killer smile, which works on her just as much as it does on every other woman Mitchell tries to charm.

"I'm just around the corner at the nurses' station if you need me," she tells him with a smile. I can't help noticing she doesn't even glance in my direction.

"It's like a super power," I say with a smirk. "No wonder it's gone to your head."

He turns back to me. "It worked, didn't it?"

"Yeah, yeah. Now help me get out of here." I fling the blanket off me, but quickly pull it back up when it registers that I'm wearing nothing but a hospital gown.

Mitchell laughs. "What do you want me to do? Help you sneak out? Your father would kill me."

"I'm going to kill you if you don't. Where are my clothes?" My eyes scan the room and fall on the chair in the far corner. A bag of personal effects is propped against the back cushion. "Grab that for me."

"You heard the nurse. The nurses' station is just around the corner. How are you going to get out of here?"

"There's nothing wrong with me. They can't keep me here."

"Maybe so, but that machine is going to go crazy the second you take those wires off you."

For a detective, he's not very observant. "Unplug it, genius."

"You're not going to let me talk you out of this, are you?"

"No. We're wasting time. I need to force another vision and find Veronica."

"Whoa." He sits down on the bed, trapping me under the blanket. "You can't seriously be thinking of doing that again. That's what landed you here."

"I don't understand why my father would bring me here. He knows how my visions work. There's nothing physically wrong with me."

"So you're saying you're mental?" he attempts a joke.

"Sort of," I say, only to take the fun out of his ribbing.

He sighs. "You were screaming your head off in the middle of the police station, and then you collapsed. Twice in two days, I caught you before you fell and really did crack open your skull. A woman in the station called an ambulance after witnessing everything. When the paramedics arrived, you weren't getting out of a trip to the ER."

"Fine, but I'm okay now, so help me get out of here." I tug on the blanket, trying to get him to move.

"You're impossible."

"I'll give you that. Now grab my clothes and turn around so I can get dressed." I push him off the bed, and thankfully, he does as I asked.

He stands near the door without it being obvious that he's standing guard. I quickly slip on my jeans, which I've been wearing for two days straight. Peeking to make sure Mitchell is still facing away from me, I quickly unplug the machine next to me, remove the wires taped to my chest, and fling the hospital gown over my head.

"Piper, we've got company. Nurse Nosy is on her way back here." Mitchell turns around, and I quickly cover my breasts. He moves toward me in a blur, grabs my shirt from the bed, and pulls it over my head. I throw my arms up into the sleeves and tug the bottom down. I don't have time to freak out over the fact that Mitchell just saw my boobs. I push him out the door, and we race down the hallway in the opposite direction of the nurse, who is screaming for us to come back.

CHAPTER THIRTEEN

We don't slow down until we're in the parking garage below the hospital and Mitchell's Explorer is in sight.

"I can't believe we just busted you out of the hospital." He pulls his keys from his jacket pocket and unlocks the car.

We get in, and he pulls out, trying to appear casual as he hands the parking ticket and a five-dollar bill to the woman in the ticket booth at the exit gate. Mitchell smiles at her and says, "Keep the change."

She blushes as she raises the gate for us.

This time I don't complain about his flirting. We need to get far away from the hospital. "So, what's the penalty for fleeing a hospital without being properly checked out?" I ask him.

"Relax. Your dad will fix this." He pulls onto the main road. "Where to? Your office?"

"No. We need to go to the station. I meant it when I said I need to see that ransom note again."

"First, you need to eat something and take a shower."

I discreetly try to sniff myself. Living in the same clothes for two days isn't exactly leaving me smelling fresh as a daisy, but I don't stink. "No time. I'll clean up once Veronica is home safe."

"From the way you screamed, Veronica needs a trip to the ER." He turns his head toward me. "Speaking of, how are you feeling?"

"Fine now." Usually sleeping after a vision that bad fixes whatever ailment I'm suffering from. I look at the clock on the dashboard. 1:17. I must have been out for about four hours.

"I'm driving you home, ordering Chinese, and telling your dad to meet us there with the ransom note." I open my mouth to protest, but Mitchell holds up his hand. "At least then, if you need to recover from whatever it is you see, you'll be in the comfort of your own home and no one will call an ambulance."

It was stupid of me to have a vision in a public place. The other police officers and detectives know about my abilities, but there were civilians around. I should have known it would end badly.

"I was careless. It's not like me, but this case is so damn frustrating."

"What's different about this case?" he asks, but his voice hitches at the end, signifying he knows the answer already.

He's what's different. In the past, it was always Dad and me working the cases together. I didn't worry about what I'd see or feel because it was only Dad. Now I have this guy watching me in my most vulnerable moments. It's affecting me. And even though we've reached an agreement and are trying to get along, it's still something that I have to get used to. I need time, but Veronica doesn't have time. Her head injury could end up causing her death if William doesn't know how to deal with it. She was knocked out by the chloroform when Rocky kicked her. Sleeping and concussions don't mix. I can't be sure she's still alive. When I notice Mitchell is still waiting for a response, I simply shrug.

Mitchell pulls up to my apartment complex and parks the car. He gets out and starts for my door, but I open it and step out.

"I just ran through a hospital and you don't think I'm okay to get out of an SUV on my own?"

He shoves his hands in his pockets. "Right." He motions for me to lead the way.

I walk up to the brown brick building and scan my key card. My apartment complex always reminded me of a college dorm. Maybe that's why it was so easy to move into after I graduated. It felt like home already. Mitchell follows me through the lobby, past the mailboxes, and to the elevator, which is conveniently open and awaiting passengers. We step inside, and I press three for my floor. Suddenly, I'm worried I left my bra draped over the kitchen chair like I sometimes do when I get home and fling the thing off immediately.

"You okay? You look a little pale," Mitchell says.

"You should probably know I'm not the neatest person."

He rubs his hands together. "I can't wait to see this. I had you pegged for a neat freak." He turns to face me with a big smile. "Tell me what I'm in for. Huge piles of laundry on the floor? Empty pizza boxes all over the kitchen counter? Unmentionables hanging in the shower?" When I don't answer he says, "That's fine. I'd rather be surprised anyway."

"Dear Lord, you aren't making it easy to be your friend."

The elevator stops at the third floor, and we step out. I point to the right and walk to the apartment at the end of the hall. I put the key in the lock and open the door.

The apartment is dark since the curtains are closed, so I

flip the light switch on the wall. The space isn't huge. Just a living room, kitchen, bathroom, and two small bedrooms, one of which I use as a home office slash library. The carpeting is off-white, and even though I hate carpeting, I can't afford to swap it out for hardwood. The rent is steep in this town. The walls are rich shades of gray, cranberry, and green. Another thing I had no say in but deal with.

"Oh come on," Mitchell says. "You got my hopes up for no reason." He walks into the kitchen, and I scurry by him to make sure my bra isn't on the kitchen chair. I breathe a sigh of relief when I see it's not. He opens the garbage can. "Even your trash is empty. Are you sure you live here?"

The truth is I spend more time at the office than at home. Mitchell doesn't need to know that about me, though. "I haven't vacuumed in a week," I offer. "And you do not want to run a white glove along my bookshelves."

He waves his hand in the air. "No one cares about that."

"Feel free to make yourself at home—within reason," I add. "The remote for the TV is on the coffee table. The fridge is pretty empty unless you like bottled water and mint chocolate chip ice cream."

His eyes light up. "Mint chocolate chip is my favorite."

"Go right ahead." I motion to the freezer drawer on my Kenmore French door refrigerator.

"Okay, but I'm ordering real food for us first."

"How much time do you think we have?" I ask. "I'm showering, and then it's back to work."

He takes me by my shoulders, spins me around, and pushes me toward the bathroom. "You're showering, eating something, and then going back to work. No discussion. Your dad will back me up on this, so you're outnumbered. Go. I'm calling him now." He nudges me inside the bathroom and shuts the door.

I open it again, and he frowns. "I need clothes. I don't exactly want to put these back on once I'm showered." I hold out my shirt, which admittedly has smelled better.

He nods and puts his phone to his ear, already calling my father.

I grab a change of clothes and take a quick shower. I'd love to stay under the steady stream of hot water for hours, but if Veronica doesn't have that luxury, then I'm sure as hell not letting myself have it either. Not until this case is over.

I walk back into the living room with my fresh clothes on and a towel wrapped around my wet hair.

"Nice look," Mitchell says with a smirk. He hands me a white cardboard container and a fork.

I take it and open it up. "How did you know I like pork lo mein?"

"I found the takeout menu in your drawer. It was circled."

"You were snooping?" I'm not totally surprised. He's a detective after all. He did a little detective work. Like me, he never really got out of the job mindset. I would have done the same in his shoes.

"Be happy I got you something you actually eat. Your dad will be here any minute."

Three soft knocks sound on my door.

I start for it, but Mitchell says, "I got it. Eat."

I sit down on the couch and dig in. I'm starving and put a heaping forkful of lo mein in my mouth, which I nearly spit right back out when Dad says, "First my daughter spends the night at your place, and then you answer her door? What the hell is going on between you two?"

"We're working a case and trying to be friends at the same time," Mitchell says, and I can't help noticing the way he's staring at his shoes instead of meeting Dad's gaze. Probably a good thing since Dad is eyeing Mitchell the same way he did my senior prom date in high school.

"Relax, Dad," I say once I've swallowed my lo mein. "Mitchell and I called a truce, and we're working overtime to solve this case. Nothing more."

He comes over and kisses the top of my head. "I had a hell of a time convincing hospital security that you legally couldn't be kept there against your will. Thank you for that. You owe me one."

"Thank you, Daddy." I give him the same smile I've used on him since I was six. "Did you bring the ransom note?" I put my food on the coffee table, but Dad picks it right back up and places it in my hand.

"After you eat."

"But—"

"I have men searching the woods around the Castells' house now. They found tracks from Rocky. So far the only tracks are from the horse. No human footprints."

"I doubt Catton would keep Veronica so close by," Mitchell says, bringing his carton of chicken and broccoli to the couch and sitting beside me. He motions for me to eat.

Dad narrows his eyes at us. "Okay, this is weird. You two getting along. Did something happen that I should know about?"

I'm not sure how to communicate that I've seen parts of Mitchell's past and I feel for the guy, so I settle for, "You were the one who asked us to get along. Mitchell doesn't want to find a different partner, and I don't want to lose my job. Simple as that." I shovel more noodles in my mouth and hold the container out to Dad.

"No thanks. I already ate." He pulls the ransom note from his pocket. "We have everyone looking for Catton and

Veronica, and I've contacted the police at UPenn as well in case they show up there."

"You may want to contact Catton's father and the Newark PD, too," I say with my mouth full.

"Already did," Dad says. "Like I said, we're doing everything we can."

Everything they can based on what I've given them, which isn't enough. I finish my food in another three bites and tilt the container toward Dad and then Mitchell, proving I ate like a good little girl. "Now hand it over," I say, wiping my mouth with a napkin.

Dad pushes the coffee table away from the couch, which earns him a look from Mitchell.

"It's in case I should collapse again," I tell him.

Mitchell nods, and I can almost see him making a mental note of such things. He really does want to make our partnership—for lack of a better word—work.

"Try to focus on Veronica, pumpkin. We know Catton is our man. We need to know where he took her. Focus on that." Dad's trying to help, but he's making me feel like a child. I know what we're looking for. I'm the one who insisted we do this. He hands me the paper, intentionally placing it in my left hand so I can decide when I want the vision to begin.

I take a deep breath, pull my legs up so I'm sitting cross-legged on the middle couch cushion, safely between Dad and Mitchell, and close my eyes before placing the note in my right hand.

Raindrops gently sprinkle the ground. Veronica's feet move slowly over the mud, rocks, and fallen leaves. And then they splash in a puddle the length of a small car. Moonlight filters through the trees, illuminating tire tracks on the ground. Tracks ending in a puddle.

Voices. Muffled voices, and then Veronica stumbles, falling face-first into the puddle.

When my eyes open, I shut them immediately. "That can't be it. It can't. I need to see more." Nothing about the trees was distinguishable. I haven't figured out anything I didn't already know.

"Pumpkin." Dad's warm hand grips my left shoulder. "What did you see?"

I look at him, conveying without words that my abilities are failing us.

"It's okay. Sometimes even the smallest detail you don't think is significant can be a big help."

I toss the ransom note aside and stand up, walking to the front window and peering out. It's been raining lightly at night lately, so I don't even know which night my vision is from. Dad's right, though. Just because I can't make sense of anything, doesn't mean he won't be able to.

"She was walking in the woods," I begin.

"So she did come to after the attack at the stables," Mitchell says, and I hear him shift on the couch, most likely to look my way.

"Yes, but she's groggy. She was walking so slowly, dragging her feet."

"Then she's leaving a trail. She might be doing it on purpose," Dad offers.

"No." It starts to rain, and I watch the drops of water hit the window and trail down the glass. "She's too weak. She fell into a big puddle. It was about eight to ten feet wide. And there were tire tracks leading into it."

"Like someone drove to that spot in the woods?" Mitchell asks, getting up and joining me at the window.

I let the curtain fall back into place. "Maybe. I don't know."

"What else did you see?" Dad asks.

"Nothing. That was it." I throw my hands up in frustration and then chew on my thumbnail.

"Okay, forget what you saw. What did you feel?" Dad continues with his usual line of questioning when I'm stumped by a vision.

"Rain."

"Did you hear anything?" Mitchell asks. "Other than rain? Did Veronica or Will say anything?"

"I heard voices, but I couldn't make them out. They were muffled, and then Veronica fell into the puddle."

"Fell or was she pushed?" Dad asks.

"I didn't feel or see anyone push her. It was more like she collapsed."

"Like you've been collapsing?" Mitchell dips his head to peer into my eyes. "Do you think you've been collapsing because Veronica is?"

First with the chloroform and now with what? "She was groggy, but maybe that wasn't from the kick to the head. What if Catton is drugging her?"

"If he got his hands on some chloroform or even made it himself..." Dad says.

"And we know he's already drugged Veronica once. At that party," Mitchell adds.

"So he's probably drugging her when he doesn't want her to see where he's taking her." I start pacing. "That would mean she's familiar with the area."

"Then you think it is somewhere around here?" Dad asks.

Mitchell shakes his head. "It can't be. Catton wouldn't know the area. He wouldn't have a place scouted out to keep her."

That's true. "I don't think it's in Philadelphia, though."

"Why?" Dad asks.

I walk into my home office and open the laptop on my desk. Dad and Mitchell follow. I pull up the weather channel and search for Philadelphia. "Here." I point to the screen. "See this band of rain. This is what's been moving through over the past few days. It's too far north of Philadelphia. They aren't getting any rain."

"So let's follow the band. The woods we're looking for have to be in that, right?" Mitchell says, dragging his finger across the screen in the same pattern as the green area marking the precipitation. He pulls out his phone. "I'm looking up parks and forests in those areas."

"But again, how would Catton know of any places to bring her?" Dad asks.

I point to Mitchell's phone. "The same way he's doing it. The information he needs is right at his fingertips."

"God, these things were so much simpler when I was younger and people didn't have the Internet in their back pockets."

I can't argue with him there, but it also means we have that same information at our fingertips. While Mitchell and Dad search for parks and forests, I head back to the living room and look at the ransom note. For the first time, I read what it says. It demands Victor Castell empty his bank account and bring the money in Veronica's black messenger bag to a PO box at the Weltunkin Post Office.

"What?" I say aloud.

"Piper, are you okay?" Dad asks, coming into the living room.

"What kind of ransom note is this? It's so amateur."

"Yeah, well I don't think Catton intended to kidnap Veronica like this. I think he was going to bring her back to school, but she got hurt and now he's panicking."

Maybe, but something feels off about this. "Catton is smart. He got into UPenn on an academic scholarship. I can't believe this is the best he could come up with."

"She's right." Mitchell comes into the living room. "I pulled up Catton's test scores from high school. The guy is like a genius. Perfect score on the SAT. Not to mention he took every test offered and aced every single one."

"It's like he was trying to prove something. Most likely because his family is poor," Dad says. "That's also motivation for turning this into a kidnapping. He needs the money."

"For what? He's already got tuition covered." Mitchell shakes his head, clearly disgusted with Catton.

Muffled voices. Voices. Plural. "Veronica wasn't talking. She was hearing the voices behind her."

Dad and Mitchell both turn to me. "What?" they ask in unison.

"Catton's not working alone. He can't be. Veronica heard people talking. Catton was either on a phone or someone else was there with them."

"So we're going back to the theory that after Catton dumped Veronica's car, someone picked him up and drove him to the spot where Veronica was being held?" Mitchell looks between Dad and me.

I nod. "Nothing else makes sense right now. And maybe Catton wasn't the one who wrote the ransom note. That could be why it doesn't sound like the work of an Ivy League student."

"So he has an idiot cousin helping him?" Mitchell's attempt at humor doesn't elicit laughter from Dad or me.

"Could be a frat buddy or someone who attended one of the fraternity's parties and became friends with Catton."

Dad huffs. "There are too many possibilities to narrow down without having more to go on."

More to go on. That's always where I come in. It's always my job to track down leads. But I've exhausted them all.

"We can check out these woods I pulled up on the map." Mitchell holds up his phone.

Looks like it's time for us to start searching on foot. "Let's go."

CHAPTER FOURTEEN

We decide to start with the woods closest to where Veronica's car was found. We know we'll have to walk a ways since they wouldn't need a car at all if the spot where they were holding her was nearby. The woods are too dense for a car to get through. We keep walking further out. Dad brought a police dog along, a German shepherd named Harry. He's trained more for finding drugs than people, but since Catton is obviously drugging Veronica, Harry might be the perfect dog for the job.

"There are some puddles up ahead here," Mitchell says off to my right. "The trees open up a bit. More sunlight is getting through."

Dad, Harry, and I race over, but the area feels foreign to me. I'd know if it was the place I saw in my vision. Harry is strictly here for sniffing out a trail I haven't seen or finding Veronica once I do locate the place in the woods from my vision. In a way, I'm just another search dog.

We look for hours, until we run out of daylight. Finally, I give up. "Let's call it quits," I yell to them. "Harry's getting hungry, and frankly so am I." I can't keep going like this when I can tell we aren't even close.

"Want to check the next area on my list?" Mitchell asks. He looks up at the lowering sun in the sky. "We could grab a bite and some flashlights and head back out."

Dad pats Harry on the head. "I've got to get him back. Let's reconvene in the morning. Six good for both of you?"

Mitchell and I nod, and we start the long trek back to the road. By the time we reach the car, we all have our phones out and are using the flashlight features on them. Harry rides shotgun, making Mitchell and I burst out laughing. We need a little comic relief right now, so I'm still smiling as we climb into the back of Dad's car.

"Hey." Mitchell nudges my leg. "You're doing great. This is a tough case, but I know we'll crack it."

"Before the deadline on the ransom note?" I ask, spinning the plain silver band I wear on my left pinky. The kidnapper said the money had to be in the PO box by Saturday. That leaves us with tomorrow to find Veronica.

"Catton must know that the cops are going to be surrounding that post office on Saturday," Mitchell says.

"Exactly. He's too smart not to know that. Which means he's either going to pull some stunt, using Veronica as a human shield to get out of there, or he's going to make contact again and make sure Victor doesn't tell us about it."

"You think he sent the first ransom note to throw *us* off?" Mitchell eyes Dad in the front seat. He's busy petting Harry, who keeps licking the side of Dad's face.

"Only one way to know. I need to pay Victor Castell a little visit." I glance at the clock on my phone. "It's only eight thirty. Care to take a little drive with me after we drop off Dad and Harry?"

"You're on." Mitchell lowers his voice even though Dad

has the radio on. "Can I ask why you want to go without your father?"

"He's tired. I can see it in his eyes. Plus, Dad likes to do everything by the book."

"And you're not planning to?" The mischievous look in Mitchell's eyes most likely matches my own.

"Not so much."

"Damn, Piper, you may cost me my badge after all."

I laugh and quickly cover my mouth to keep from drawing Dad's attention. "Only if you're dumb enough to get caught."

The look on his face is nothing short of *Challenge accepted.*

Twenty minutes later, Dad and Harry are back at the station and Mitchell and I are on our way to the Castells' house. I don't call to let them know we're coming—something Dad would have insisted upon. I want to catch them off guard. I want to see what it is they're hiding. I've already figured out Victor's feelings for his daughter aren't greater than his love of his money. If he was so good at hiding that, he could definitely be hiding more, including another ransom note.

There are exactly two lights on in the Castell house when we pull up the driveway. One in the downstairs room near the garage, and the other an upstairs bedroom in the middle of the house. I'm willing to bet that's the master bedroom, and most likely Darla Castell is occupying it at the moment. If I had to guess, I'd say the downstairs room is a study or office of some nature, and Victor Castell is inside.

"Do we ring the bell?" Mitchell asks. "Or are you going to pull out a Cat Woman suit and scale the side of the house so you can climb in through one of the three balconies?

Because if that's the route we're going, you should have told me to wear different shoes."

"Fine, we'll do it the civilian way. You're no fun at all, though. I'm not even sure I can return the Cat Woman costume."

He bumps his shoulder against mine and rings the bell.

I allow myself the whole twenty seconds it takes Victor Castell to answer the door to reflect on how nice it is to talk to someone on a human level. Someone other than my parents and Marcia.

Victor pulls the door open, adjusting a pair of reading glasses on his nose. "Detectives?" He consults his diamond-encrusted watch. "Did we have an appointment?"

Mitchell's quick sideways glance in my direction leads me to believe he's willing to go along with the lie, but I don't think we'll get anywhere that way.

"No, Mr. Castell. Detective Brennan and I stopped by because we have some information about your daughter's case and we assumed you'd want to be kept up-to-date."

Victor nods. "Of course. I was just in my study going over my bank statement. Please, come in." He steps aside, allowing us to pass.

"Your bank statement?" I ask him, stopping in the foyer as he closes the door. "Are you preparing to pay the ransom fee in exchange for your daughter? I was under the impression you froze all your bank accounts."

Victor laces his fingers in front of him. "Not all of my accounts. Don't take this the wrong way, Detectives, but the Saturday deadline is fast approaching. Unless you are here to tell me you know where my daughter is being held and you have dispatched a team to bring her home..." He lets the rest of the sentence trail off.

"So, you're convinced we'll fail." Mitchell crosses his

arms, his pectoral muscles flexed. He's clearly trying to intimidate the slender Victor Castell, but the truth is, Victor is right. He opens his mouth to speak, but I hold up a hand.

"Mr. Castell, you said you were in your study?"

He dips his head forward once, which I take as affirmation.

"May we talk there?"

His brow furrows. "Why?"

"Because I believe you aren't being completely honest with us. I think the ransom note you turned over to the police department isn't the only communication you've had with the kidnapper. Is that true?" I don't cross my arms like Mitchell. I let my words take Victor down a notch.

He swallows hard, and his adam's apple bobs. "I..." He shakes his head, like he can't bear to continue.

I look at Mitchell, trying to silently communicate what I'm about to do. I'll need him to have my back since I have no way of knowing what I'm about to see. I step forward and place my right hand on Victor's arm, just above his elbow in a reassuring way. "I promise we—"

"You can't bring that to the police! You'll get her killed," Darla Castell yells.

Victor looks up at her from his desk in the study. "You expect me to transfer the money, no questions asked? What was the point of enlisting the WPD's help if we're simply going to meet the kidnapper's demands?"

Darla walks around the mahogany desk to her husband's side. "Simple. We didn't know if she was kidnapped or if she simply took off in a fit again. But now we know. We have no choice. Do you want your daughter to die after all we've...?" She turns away from him and walks over to the bookshelf that lines the far wall.

"Then we'll keep this a secret. If the police don't find her by Thursday night, I'll prepare the funds for transfer."

Darla nods but doesn't turn around. "If only you hadn't asked her to come home this weekend. She'd be at school. Safe."

"You blame me?" The pen slips from Victor's hand.

Darla turns around, her steely gaze falling on her husband. "You don't?"

"How was I to know something like this would happen? Veronica has come home every year on my birthday."

"Only she didn't want to this year." Darla moves toward Victor. "You insisted. Whatever's happened is on your head."

My hand is ripped free of Victor's arm, and Mitchell immediately pulls me behind him. Does he think Victor will do something to retaliate after my intrusion of his private memories?

"What did you just do?" Victor's eyes are cold and full of hate as he rubs his arm where I just touched him.

"Piper?" Mitchell asks, still shielding me.

"It's fine." I step out from behind Mitchell. "Mr. Castell, I'm sorry, but you hired me to find your daughter and that's exactly what I'm trying to do."

"My husband hired the WPD, not *you*, Ms. Ashwell." Darla's voice couldn't be filled with more hatred as she descends the staircase in the front hall.

"The WPD hired Ms. Ashwell," Mitchell offers in my defense.

I hold my hands up in front of me to put an end to the conversation. "Are you people serious? Do you want to find your daughter or not?" My eyes flit back and forth between Victor and Darla, landing on Darla. "You blame him for Veronica's disappearance, don't you? You think it's his fault since he asked her to come home. You're the reason he hid the second ransom note."

"The second one?" Mitchell asks.

"Yes," Victor says. "We received two communications."

"Can we see the second one?" Mitchell asks, adding, "Please."

Victor and Darla exchange a look, one I can't interpret without coming into physical contact with one of them. "This way." He holds his hand out. "My study is this way."

I go first with Mitchell staying directly behind me. The study is large, more like a school library than a room in someone's house. I go directly to the desk I saw in my vision. My eyes falling on the laptop in the center. A bankbook sits next to it. Do people still use those?

Darla walks over and flips the book closed before I can read any numbers. "All you need to see is the message we received." She picks up a paper and holds it out to me. I can't help noticing she's being careful not to touch me. She must have witnessed me reading her husband and doesn't want to fall victim to my abilities the way he did.

The paper is a printout of an email, which means I can't use my ability to get a read off of it. However, it does give instructions for transferring the money into a bank account, so we can use that information. I know it's a long shot, but I ask, "Would you mind us taking a look at your email itself."

"I don't see why that's necessary," Darla says. "This is all we've gotten. And I see no reason why you need to snoop into our personal business."

At the mention of business, I double-check the email address the note was sent to. "Mr. Castell, the kidnapper sent this to your personal email, not a work email address."

"Yes." He gives me a quizzical look.

"Well," Mitchell says, "if the kidnapper was after

your money and knew of your business dealings, they'd more likely send the email to a business address."

"How would they get your personal address? That's the real question Detective Brennan is asking." I address Victor, but it's Darla who answers me.

"You think this person knows us?"

"Mrs. Castell, we believe your daughter's..." What do I call Will? Boyfriend doesn't seem right. I settle on "Friend, William Catton got into an argument with her on Friday night and may have come here on Saturday to bring her back to school."

"Why wouldn't she just tell us?" Victor asks.

Darla sits down at Victor's desk, a forlorn expression washing over her features. "I warned her to stay away from that boy."

"You know him?" I ask, moving toward her.

She nods. "Veronica told me about him. He's a nasty boy. Truly disrespectful."

"Do you know he drugged your daughter the night they met?" I ask.

"No!" Victor practically yells. "Veronica would have told us if something like that had happened."

Would she? The Castells have been trying to keep their daughter's disappearance out of the media. My instinct tells me they'd cover up any mess she got into with a fraternity boy as well. "Perhaps she didn't think she could come to you about it."

"What are you implying?" Victor moves toward me, but Mitchell holds up a hand to stop him.

"We are just asking questions in the hopes of finding answers," Mitchell tells him.

"Actually..." Darla stands up again and faces the bookshelf, most likely so she doesn't have to look at her husband. "Veronica did come to me."

Victor tries to step forward, but Mitchell's still at the ready and motions for him to let his wife speak.

"She said she drank too much at a party. She's underage. I couldn't let her go to the authorities. They'd do a full drug test. Besides, she knew what Will had done." Darla turns around. "I offered him money, thinking that's what he was after."

"Money for what?" I ask. "The video he made of your daughter?"

"Video?" Victor's face turns red. "Video of what?"

Darla looks to me, and I don't know if she isn't privy to all the details or if she doesn't have the courage to tell her husband.

"Apparently, Veronica put on a show for the fraternity. Will wanted her to 'entertain'"—I pause to make air quotes—"some rushees last weekend. That's what they fought about."

"And you think he came here and forced her to go back to school with him?"

"I think that was the plan, but she refused."

"So he took her by force," Mitchell finishes for me. "Only, he didn't return to school because there was an accident and Veronica was injured." He fills them in on the incident at the stables.

"So where did he bring her?" Darla asks.

"That's the question," I say. "We initially thought he must be nearby if he wants us to bring the money to the local post office." I hold up the printed email. "But this email with the change of plans means he could be anywhere."

"What do we do?" Darla asks. "Should Victor email him

back? Try to get him to agree to the original location of the drop off?"

It's clear the post office was a sham to keep the WPD busy. Will would never agree to that. "No. But we do need you to get him talking."

"I need to lie down," Darla says. "This is all too much." She starts for the door. "Victor, you'll take care of this?"

He nods and watches her leave the room. "What's our next move?"

"May I?" I motion to his computer.

He walks over to the laptop and brings up his email. "There." On the screen he has the email from Will. "That's the only communication I've gotten electronically."

I'd love for him to step away so I can confirm that by scanning his inbox and deleted files, but he watches me like a hawk. I click reply on the email and motion for Mitchell to join me on this side of the desk. My fingers hover over the keys as I contemplate my response.

I can't get my bank to transfer that much money at once. Given the nature of my business, I have taken certain precautions and set limitations on the amount that can be withdrawn or transferred at one time. I can transfer a third of the amount and bring the rest to you in person in exchange for my daughter. I don't care who you are. I just want my daughter returned. No police. Just me, you, and Veronica. Name the time and place.

There's a major flaw with my plan, and Catton should be smart enough to see it. If there are limits to how much can be withdrawn, Victor Castell wouldn't be able to make the deadline regardless of the method of delivery. My hope is that he's panicked and either won't figure that out, or he'll offer an extension for the rest of the money, buying us time to find him.

Mitchell reads over my shoulder, and I know he's picked up on my plan. Instead of nodding or verbalizing his approval, he simply presses send.

I'm surprised when an answer comes almost immediately.

Wire a third of the money now and another third tomorrow. I'll accept the final payment on Saturday. No in-person meeting. Once I'm paid in full, I'll email you instructions for how you can find Veronica.

Mitchell slams an open palm against the desk, which makes Victor jump. "What is it?" Victor asks.

"Just hang on." I press reply.

My bank won't permit three transfers in three days. I need more time.

I press send and wait, tapping my fingers on the desk and refreshing the email inbox every few seconds. I take the time to scan the other emails, but there's not much. Victor keeps a tidy inbox. Other than an invite to the opening of a new country club and a notification that his phone bill is ready for viewing and payment, his inbox is empty.

"What's taking him so long to respond this time?" Mitchell asks, worry lines deepening in his forehead.

"Maybe he's trying to figure out his next move. Bank policies are stymieing his plans."

A new message appears in the inbox, and I immediately click on it. Mitchell and Victor huddle around the screen to read it along with me.

Each day I don't get a third of the money, Veronica loses an appendage. I'm guessing she'll bleed out long before anyone discovers her body.

CHAPTER FIFTEEN

I throw my keys on the kitchen counter and put on a pot of coffee for Mitchell and me. Right after we got Catton's response, Victor called Darla back into the study. As soon as she read the email, she went into a full-on panic attack, and Victor excused himself to give her a tranquilizer—something she apparently has a prescription for since she's prone to attacks like this.

I called Dad on the way back to my apartment and filled him in. Naturally, he wasn't happy Mitchell and I decided to visit the Castells unannounced and without him present. But he's already looking into the email address Catton is using and how to get our hands on enough money to keep Veronica alive until we find her.

"What about counterfeit money?" Mitchell asks, leaning against my kitchen counter. "If Catton tries to use it, we could easily have it traced."

"That could work." I take two mugs out of the cabinet above the stove and place them on the countertop much rougher than necessary.

"Easy there," Mitchell says.

"Sorry. I'm just frustrated. I should have found Veronica by now."

"You know who took her, when he took her, and that he's keeping her in the woods somewhere. You're three for three. Cut yourself some slack."

"You don't get it." He can't because this is the first case he's worked on with me. Before this one, he and I would run into each other at the station, but that was it.

"I've read every report from every case you've worked on. I know we're on a time crunch, but we're going to find this guy and Veronica." He smirks, which I find very odd until he says, "You know the saying: a vision a day keeps the killer away."

"That is the worst joke ever," I say.

He shrugs. The coffee pot gives three short beeps, indicating the coffee is finished brewing. He reaches for the pot and pours us two mugs as if he's always done so.

I cock my head at him. "Why are you suddenly so comfortable around me?" I gesture to the coffee pot he's returning to the hot plate.

He rubs his forehead. "Promise you won't laugh?"

"Not at all." I cross my arms in front of my chest, challenging him to tell me anyway.

"I guess I should expect that from you. Banter is our thing, right?" His bluntness is refreshing. It's safe. Free of emotions I don't deal with well.

I pick up a mug and sip the coffee. "Wouldn't have it any other way."

"Okay, when you have your visions, it makes me think of my mom. At first, it was difficult for me, and I tried to distance myself from you to make it easier. But now that you know the truth about her... I don't know. I guess I feel closer to you. Like I can tell you just about anything." He looks down at his black coffee, and the awkward silence that ensues is too much for me.

"Please don't," I say. "I'm afraid to know what's rattling around in that mind of yours most of the time."

He laughs. "Right now it's that I'd love some creamer for this."

"Sorry, but if it's not ice cream or cheese, I don't do dairy."

"Do you still have that mint chocolate chip ice cream?" He starts for the freezer before he finishes getting the words out.

"Help yourself." He already seems to be making himself at home. I open the cabinet above the coffee pot and take out a bowl.

"Don't bother," he says, grabbing the half gallon. "This is going in my coffee."

"I'm not sure if you're disgusting or a total genius for wanting to try that."

"Let's find out, shall we?" he says with a huge smile as he removes the lid from the container.

I grab two spoons from the silverware drawer and hand him one. We each take a scoop and drop it into our mugs, swirling the spoons to mix the ice cream into the hot coffee.

"On three?" he asks.

I shake my head. "Too much time to rethink this." I lift my mug. "Bottoms up."

He smirks and brings his mug to his mouth.

In a word, it's...different. Like mint mocha. The odd part is the chocolate chips, which haven't completely melted yet. I chew one with exaggerated effort. "Crunchy."

"I like it," he says, taking another sip.

"So, back to the case. There's something that's bothering me."

"Only one thing?" He eyes me over the mug as he continues to drink.

"Well, no, but I can't help wondering what happened to Veronica's phone. I would think a college student would carry their phone at all times, right?"

"It's like an appendage for most people, regardless of age. My grandmother even has a smart phone." He winks to show he's only kidding about that last part.

"Okay, so why can't we get the phone company to trace hers? It wasn't in her car or her room, so she must have had it the day she was abducted."

Mitchell pulls out his phone. "I'm texting your dad to tell him to check."

I lean against the refrigerator. "Should we feel bad we keep making him do all the research?"

"Nah. We're doing the fieldwork, so it's only fair."

Somehow I don't think Dad will see it that way. Still, he has the most experience and the most contacts to call in favors with.

"Okay, he already texted back. They tried to track the phone when they checked the call records. Apparently, the phone's last known whereabouts were at the Castells' house."

"Last known? What does that mean?" I ask, taking another sip of my coffee concoction and then putting it aside for a fresh cup.

Mitchell laughs. "Didn't like it, huh?"

"I just prefer the real stuff." I grab a new mug and pour the steamy hot liquid into it. "Back to the phone."

"Right. It looks like the phone was destroyed."

"On the premises?"

He nods.

"So Will must have destroyed it at the stables after

Veronica was kicked in the head by the horse." I hold my mug tightly in my hands and breathe in the aroma.

"Are you smelling your coffee?" Mitchell quirks a brow at me.

"Yeah, sorry. I try to tap into all my senses. It calms me and helps me remember things I might have overlooked." I start to lower the mug, but he quickly intercepts, raising it back to my face.

"Don't stop on my account. You don't have to be self-conscious or embarrassed about your abilities in front of me." He leans back against the island counter across from me. "The more I'm around you, the more I realize my mother's visions weren't so subtle." He has a far off look in his eyes, so I remain silent, letting him continue in his own time.

"She used to stare out the kitchen window when she washed the dishes. I never understood why she insisted on washing them by hand when we had a dishwasher, but I think in a way she found the process relaxing."

The warm water, the bubbly soap suds, the sounds of the liquids being washed down the drain... All sensations that probably helped her center herself.

His gaze shifts, and he stares at me for a moment. "You do the same thing, don't you?"

I nod.

He suddenly stands up straight and moves toward my sink. "Hey, you said you heard rain in the woods, right?"

"Yeah. It's rained several nights here, though. And rain doesn't help me find this place. It can't allow me to distinguish between one set of trees and another."

"But could a similar sound help you focus on that vision and maybe see more?" He turns on the faucet, setting the flow to a trickle.

"I won't see anything I haven't already seen, but I should be able to picture it again. Or at the very least hear it."

He takes me by my shoulders and places me directly in front of the sink. This sort of contact with another human being who isn't one of my parents is still odd for me. For most of my life, I've shied away from human contact. I didn't have my first kiss until I was eighteen. And I saw more of that poor guy's life in those twenty seconds than he probably ever wanted to share with anyone. Now, ten years later, I'm better at controlling my visions. But I still don't make contact with others often. Mostly out of habit.

"You okay?" Mitchell asks me. "Do you sense anything?"

I shake my head. "Not yet." I don't want to tell him what I was busy thinking about, so I focus my attention on the water. The stream is too steady though. I lower the pressure, letting the water come out in distinct drips and drops, much like rain. I recall the image of the woods, the sound of the murmured voices, the feel of the cold rain on my skin. Wait! That wasn't the rain that just hit my neck—Veronica's neck.

I turn around, my eyes wide. "Right before Veronica fell into the puddle, someone stuck a needle into her neck."

"So Catton *is* drugging her. Repeatedly." He roughs up the sides of his hair and lets out a frustrated growl. "I really want to get my hands on this guy."

"Except you don't want to lose your badge, so you're going to have to calm down." I want to lock Will Catton up as much as Mitchell does, but I can see he wants to take a few good swings at the guy first.

But once again, my visions aren't showing me anything I

can use. Everything I know to be true isn't showing me where Catton took Veronica. Unless... "Tire marks."

"What?" Mitchell stops clenching his fists.

"I saw tire marks leading into the puddle. They must be from the car Catton used to bring Veronica into the woods. I think I could try to sketch them." I open the kitchen drawer and remove a small pad and pencil.

"You draw?" Mitchell looks over my shoulder.

"Only from visions. And it's not a typical method of drawing either."

"What do you mean?"

It's easier to show him, so I position my pencil over the pad and close my eyes. I take three deep breaths, centering myself as I call up the image of the puddle. My hand starts to move over the paper.

"Holy crap," Mitchell mutters over my shoulder.

I force his voice from my mind and continue to draw. When I'm finished, I open my eyes and look down at the paper.

"That's incredible. You could do sketches for the Weltunkin PD."

I shake my head and flip to the next sheet of paper on the pad. "Give me an animal."

"What?"

"Just name an animal."

"A bunny."

I gawk at him. "Really? Tough Mitchell Brennan's first thought when I tell him to name an animal is a cute little bunny?"

"Who said anything about cute? This bunny is rabid and ready to tear you to shreds." He smirks, but I'm not buying it.

"Whatever. Doesn't matter anyway. Watch." With my

eyes open, I try my best to sketch a simple bunny, but it looks more like a demented snowman.

"You're pulling my leg, right?" he says when I finish and turn the paper to face him.

"Not even a little. I can only draw from my visions." I flip back to the image of the tire tracks. "We need to find out what kind of tires leave marks like this. I'm assuming that will tell us what kind of car Catton is using. He's too smart to use his own."

"But you said he never meant to take this to the level of kidnapping. That thought came after Veronica was kicked in the head."

He's right, but something gave me this idea, so it has to mean something. "I can't always explain why I get these ideas, but there always important in some way."

Without needing further explanation, Mitchell nods, rips the paper from the pad, and starts for my home office. "You don't mind, do you?"

I follow him and chuckle. "Now you ask, after you've already made yourself at home here?"

He stops walking and turns back to me. "Sorry. I didn't—"

I hold up my hand to stop him. "It's fine. Really. In a way, it makes me feel almost normal, having someone over here and not totally uncomfortable in my living space." I'm not sure why I'm admitting these personal things to him. Maybe I feel like I owe him for the times I read him against his will. Either way, he doesn't press me for more information. It's odd how well we are getting along now that we tore down the walls we immediately erected upon meeting.

We spend the next few hours searching for the tires on the vehicle Catton used. We call Dad and update him as well. By the time we're finished, it's two in the morning.

Friday morning. Our last day to find Veronica before Will starts bleeding her dry.

I don't remember falling asleep or moving to the living room, but I wake up at seven to the sound of my iPhone ringing on the coffee table. Blinking, I reach for the phone and press the speaker button to answer the call. "Hello?"

"We got the car," Dad's voice says.

I bolt upright on the couch, my back aching in protest. "Already?"

Mitchell rubs the sleep from his eyes and attempts to sit up straight in the chair. From the contorted look of pain on his face, he's in worse shape than I am.

"It's an old Ford Fusion. Turns out it's registered to Jeremy Schmidt, Will's stepfather, so no surprise there. But the good news is we put the word out to hunt down this vehicle and guess what?"

"You found it already?"

"And you're not going to believe where."

Without thinking, I answer, "In a body of water."

Mitchell cocks his head at me the same time Dad says, "How did you know?"

"The giant puddle I saw. I don't think it was actually from the woods. I think I was seeing two images at the same time. Like they were overlapping." It's happened before. It's why I refer to my visions as whispers. Sometimes they come to me from more than one direction, like standing in the middle of a crowd and trying to make out the different conversations happening simultaneously.

"So you're saying the car was found in a lake?" Mitchell asks.

"Seriously?" Dad says. "You're there again?"

I don't dare tell Dad Mitchell stayed over at my place, not after how he reacted to me spending the night at

Mitchell's the last time. "Today's our final day to solve this case," I say. "No time to waste." Technically not a lie, though it's not the correct answer to Dad's question at all.

"Lake Harmon, right outside Weltunkin Park," Dad says.

I put the phone back on the coffee table. "So those are the woods we need to search." I'm already up and heading to my bedroom to change. I can hear Dad and Mitchell talking while I pull on clean clothes and a jacket. When I return, Mitchell hands my phone to me.

"He's meeting us there." His jacket is on, and he's ready to go. "I called Marcia. She's getting three coffees and a few muffins ready for us. We'll stop on the way."

Mitchell drives, and when he pulls up to Marcia's Nook, she's already outside with the cardboard drink holder and a to-go bag. She brings the order to my window so I don't even have to get out of the car. "Thanks, Marcia. Put it on my tab and throw in a nice tip for yourself."

"Not a chance. Consider it my contribution to the Weltunkin PD."

Mitchell gives her a nod, and we pull out of the parking lot. "She's pretty great," he says.

"She's single," I tell him, realizing they might actually make a good couple. Now that I know there's more to him, he might be the kind to actually settle into a committed relationship.

"She's perfect too, the right combination of sexy and adorable. That's hard to find."

I pull a coffee from the holder and hand it to him. "Want me to set it up for you?" He gives me a sideways glance. "Not that you need my help getting a date," I add.

"It's not that. Marcia is amazing. Any guy would be lucky to have her, but I'd never date her."

"Why not?"

"You and I are a lot alike. We're both the job. Look at me. I spent the night on the chair in your living room. I haven't showered, and I'm wearing the same clothes I wore yesterday. What woman would willingly commit to this lifestyle?"

I take a sip of my coffee, unable to argue because I know exactly what he means. I love my job more than I can see myself loving a man.

We don't talk for the rest of the way to Lake Harmon, but it's not an awkward silence. It's peaceful, and it gives me a chance to sort through my visions. The voices I heard could have been from the lake and not the woods. Maybe whoever was helping Catton ditched the car for him while Catton took Veronica the rest of the way on foot. I should know once I see the car and the lake. There should be enough for me to read and get some concrete answers.

We spot Dad as we pull up. The Weltunkin PD has a tow truck on the edge of the lake, and attached to the back of it is a silver Ford Fusion. I hand the coffee holder and muffin bag to Mitchell as soon as he cuts the engine. He doesn't say a word as he takes it from me, and I get out of the car. Dad knows not to interrupt me either. He just watches as I approach the car. But before I get to it, something makes me turn toward the lake.

I move past Dad to the edge of the lake and bend down next to the tall grass.

"What is she—?" Mitchell asks, and without turning, I know Dad's stopped him.

I pluck a single blade of grass from the patch and stand up. It glistens in the early morning sunlight, a combination of dew and dried red blood.

"It's Veronica's blood," I say.

CHAPTER SIXTEEN

"Get the dogs here," Dad tells another officer on site.

"Can you read it?" Mitchell asks, suddenly right next to me.

"Yeah. I can."

He places a reassuring hand on my shoulder, which earns us both a look of confusion from my father. He's used to seeing me pull away from people, yet here I am letting someone I seemed to hate just days earlier touch me when I'm about to have a vision.

My intake of air is shaky, the anticipation of what I'm about to see sending my nerves into hyper drive. Will threatened to bleed Veronica. Has he already? Was saying that just a cover-up for the horrors he's already committed. I turn to Mitchell. "There's a good chance what I see and feel is going to send me falling into this lake. Don't let them take me to the hospital. Do you hear me? I need to find her. Now. Whether she's alive or not, this is ending today."

"What are you asking me to do, Piper?" Mitchell searches my eyes, looking for some clarity to my words.

"Catch me when I fall." My eyes flit in Dad's direction.

"And wake me up by any means necessary before he loses it and takes me off this case."

"Has he done that before?" Mitchell whispers.

"He's tried." I give a half-hearted smile.

"I've got your back." His hand squeezes mine. It happens so fast I'm not sure if I imagined it.

"Thank you." I haven't been in a position to say that to anyone in a really long time. "You ready?"

"You've got this," he says, and I can tell he's talking to himself as much as he is to me.

I meet Dad's gaze and nod. He hates this. I know the reason he always brings me in on cases is so he can watch over me. He hates it when people come to me on their own, without going through him first. He's always been the protective father, and no matter how old I get, that's not going to change. He looks to Mitchell, and the expression on his face is clear. He trusts Mitchell. It all becomes crystal clear. The real reason he agreed to let Mitchell be his partner after Dad worked alone for so many years. It wasn't just because Mitchell was interested in my abilities. It's because Dad trusts him and thinks Mitchell will protect me. Dad can retire, having already put in his time on the force. He's grooming Mitchell as his replacement. A single tear escapes my eye as that knowledge sets in.

"Piper?" Mitchell asks.

"I'm okay." I'm just missing my dad, even though he's not officially gone yet. We've been a team for years. I'm going to miss that, but it also makes sense now why he's allowed Mitchell and me to go off on our own without much complaint. He hoped we'd start getting along the way we have. In a way, his absence forced us to.

"Love you, Dad," I mouth to him.

"Love you, pumpkin," he mouths back. It was what he used to say when I was twelve and my visions first started.

I close my eyes and allow the vision to fill me.

Veronica opens her eyes, the night sky dark and difficult to see with the cloud cover. Gurgling sounds nearby fill her ears. Her head pounds, specifically where Rocky's hoof connected with her temple, but there's something else too. Her thoughts are cloudy, hazy. The effects of the drugs haven't worn off. Tears trickle down her face, but she can't wipe them because something is restraining her hands. She twists her wrists, and the soft fabric rubs against her skin. It feels like a shirt or maybe a scarf. Definitely a scarf. She keeps tugging, trying to force her hands apart behind her back. She twists on the ground and the image of the silver Ford comes into focus as she turns her head to the left. The car is sinking into the river. The car where she was forced into the trunk. The panic of waking up in total darkness, the feeling of the ground moving beneath her...

Veronica starts to scream. Voices sound, but they aren't discernable over her yelling. And then something metal connects with the side of her head.

I'm on the ground in Mitchell's arms when I come to.

"You've got to stop doing this to me," he tells me when my eyes open and focus on him.

"At least we know you can follow directions," I tease. "You caught me."

Dad is squatting down beside us, and he gives me a curious look. "You okay?"

"Yeah." I sit up with Mitchell's help. "There should be more blood. Will hit her with something metal. I never saw him because Veronica didn't see him. She was knocked out on the ground, but she came to and she started to scream.

"He doesn't have her gagged to stop her from doing that?" Mitchell asks. "I thought the kid was supposed to be smart."

"He's drugging her. She's unconscious most of the time. He only wakes her up when he needs her to move on her own. He transported her in the trunk of the car."

"Did he carry her after he knocked her out again here?" Dad asks. "He ditched the car, so how else would he get around."

A patrol car pulls up, and an officer with a police dog gets out. He walks over to my father. "Detective, Harry's ready for duty." He hands Harry's leash to Dad.

"Thanks, Wallace," Dad says, before he bends down to pet Harry's head.

I extend the blade of grass with Veronica's blood on it to Harry. "Here you go, boy. Find Veronica."

Harry sniffs the grass and then immediately turns toward the shoreline. After a few seconds, he starts barking furiously.

"What do you smell, boy?" Mitchell whispers beside me, not wanting to disturb Harry's concentration.

I move around him and bend down where Harry has his nose pressed to the dirt. Harry paws at it, indicating he wants to dig. He waits for me to give a nod before proceeding. With one careful and practiced paw, Harry digs up the dirt. He puts his nose in the hole and sniffs. Then he moves closer to the water's edge.

"It's possible whatever he smells was washed into the lake by the rain," I say. "Anyone have a shovel?"

The guy with the tow truck reaches into the vehicle and produces a tire wrench. "Would this work?" he asks, holding it up.

As soon as I see it, my hand goes to my temple. "That's

what Veronica was hit with in my vision."

Mitchell moves toward the tow truck operator, misinterpreting my words.

"No, I don't mean that exact one. But that was the weapon. A tire wrench." I look down at the ground by the edge of the water. "Did they toss it into the water? Is that what you smell, Harry?" It has to be. The scent of Veronica's blood drew Harry here. It would make sense that the instrument Will used to knock her out had blood on it since he hit her where she was already injured. He probably threw it in the water with the hope that the blood would be washed away.

"This poor girl needs medical attention ASAP," Dad says. "If she's even still alive."

"Catton obviously has drugs, but do you think he's also giving her something to ensure she stays alive? If she dies, he doesn't get paid."

Mitchell shakes his head and looks out over the water. "No. Catton said he'd give Castell the directions to find Veronica *after* he got his money. He could easily let her die. In fact, it would be easier for him if he did."

God, that's true. "We don't have time to debate this. They're in these woods somewhere. We need more dogs and more men out here. Surround the woods." I start toward the car and stare at the trunk. She was in there. "Open the trunk," I tell the guy with the tow truck.

"I don't have keys. The car is locked."

I grab the tire wrench from his hand and smash the front driver's side window. Dad groans, not happy I'm messing with police evidence, but I don't care. I need to get inside that trunk and feel what Veronica felt. Hopefully hear something. Reaching through the window, I unlock the car. Then I get inside, sitting in the driver's seat. Before I can even find the trunk latch, I feel something. Waves of nausea course through me, and I clutch my stomach.

"Piper," Dad says. "Don't fight the vision. You know it only makes it worse."

But this one feels so...vile. I look at my father, my eyes pleading with his. There have only been a few times in my life when I've wished I could give up my abilities. Those times were when I found dead bodies. Those were the times I experienced the people I was looking for dying. Usually brutally. "Dad," is all I can manage to choke out.

He places his hand against my cheek, which is moist from my tears. "I know, pumpkin. I know. I'll stay right here. I'm with you."

The passenger door opens, and Mitchell sits next to me. "So am I, Piper. We're in this together." He looks at my father. "All of us."

I know what I need to do. The vision I had inside Veronica's car, the one that drew me to the steering wheel...it wasn't because I was supposed to read *that* steering wheel. I'm supposed to read this one. It's why I saw Will's driving gloves. It was trying to tell me to read his car. I reach my right hand for the steering wheel, my fingers shaking until they wrap around the two o'clock position. I allow my eyes to close.

Will is sitting in the back seat. I can see him in the rearview mirror. He's tied up, his shaggy blond hair is disheveled, and his eyes are full of fear. "Listen, man, I don't give a shit what you do to her. I don't know who the hell you are, so just let me go."

"You keep yapping and I'm going to do one of two things: gag you or shut you up for good. Got it?" The voice is deep, almost gravelly.

Will nods, his bottom lip quivering. "I can help you. Untie me, and I'll help you."

"You are helping already," the man says. "Veronica told her mother about you. It's no secret you've been making her do things. Things she didn't want to do. Now you get into a fight, which her mother overhears, and you show up here."

"What are you saying? Are you trying to pin all this on me?" Will thrashes against the back seat. "You're the one who locked her in the goddamn trunk."

The man driving the car laughs. "Tell it to the police."

"I will." The look in Will's eyes indicates he knows his mistake as soon as the words leave his mouth. "No! I didn't mean that. Please, just let me go. I'll go back to school, and I won't say a word about any of this."

The car bumps on the uneven terrain. It's too dark to make out the surroundings, though.

This time the man doesn't answer Will, which sends Will into a panic. He raises his legs and kicks at the back of the guy's seat.

"That's it!" The man stops the car and gets out. All the while, Will is pleading for his life. The man pulls open Will's door and grabs for him, but Will is kicking his legs, fighting back. Will tries to scramble for the opposite door, but with his hands tied behind his back, he can't get the door open. He continues to kick, but the guy grabs one leg. He pulls a pocketknife out of the back pocket of his jeans and slices Will's Achilles tendon. Will cries out in pain, and the guy slams the door shut to muffle the screams. Then he walks around to the other side of the car, opens the door, grabs Will by his hair, and raises the knife. "Shut up now, or I'll plunge this knife into your eye," he practically growls.

Will bites his lip to keep from screaming.

"On second thought..." The man raises the knife in the air and brings it down before Will can even try to scramble away.

When I stop screaming, I'm on the grass about twenty feet from the car. Dad must have pulled me out to stop the vision. He's been known to do that, which is something I both love him for and hate as a PI. My body is contorted, one hand gripping my Achilles on my left leg and the other pressed against my right eye.

"Piper. It's over. It's okay." Dad's voice is soothing but loud. He knows I'm no longer locked inside the vision, but he also knows the aftereffects can linger for quite some time.

"I think it's pretty safe to assume Veronica Castell is dead," Mitchell says, and I look up at him to see he's on the phone.

"No," I choke out. "Not her."

"Who? You saw someone else?" Dad asks. "Is there another missing person we don't know about?"

"Catton. He's dead." I stop clutching my ankle and lower my hand.

"Veronica?" Dad asks, assuming she somehow got the upper hand and took out her abductor.

"Someone else. I saw the vision through his eyes, so I don't know what he looks like. I caught a little of his reflection in the car windows."

"Can you sketch him?" Mitchell asks me, squatting down and reaching for his pad in his jacket pocket.

"She's too shaken up right now," Dad says. "Give her a minute." He turns his attention back to me. "Piper, can you tell us what he looked like?"

"He looked to be in his fifties, and he has a beard." That's all I can tell you.

"Who is he? Was he helping Catton? Could it be his

father?"

I sit up more and see the other officers are searching the lake. Most likely for the tire wrench used on Veronica. "Catton didn't know the guy. He said Veronica was locked in the trunk. He offered to help the man in exchange for his freedom—said he didn't care what he did to Veronica."

"So, let me get this straight," Mitchell says. "Catton kidnapped Veronica, and then he was also kidnapped by someone else kidnapping Veronica? The kidnapper got kidnapped?"

He's right. It's completely crazy. But now things are actually starting to make sense. My visions were trying to let me know I needed to find and help William Catton, too. In their own cryptic way, as usual. That's why they were honed in on Will more than Veronica. Because Will was going to die first.

"We're searching for Will's body. It might be in there," I say, pointing to the lake. My eyes return to the car. "Or in there." The trunk. Veronica was in the trunk. "Open the trunk. Now!"

Dad helps me up as Mitchell rushes to get the trunk open.

"Are we hoping to find Catton or Veronica in here?" he asks.

"Will," I answer. I peer into the back seat of the car. "There should be blood everywhere. Why isn't there any blood?" I close my eyes and try to picture the horrific scene again. "Slip covers. There were slip covers on the seat."

"Got it," Mitchell calls to us as he lifts the lid on the trunk with a small crowbar in his hand. "I found the slip covers." He covers his mouth and nose. "I'm guessing this is William Catton." He steps back, waiting for Dad and me to join him.

I hold my breath as I take the three steps around the back of the car. Will is partially wrapped in the seat cover. The man who killed him must have used the material to transport the body. Will's face is frozen in a look of horror. Only one eye stares back at us. The other is mutilated. How many times did the man stab him?

Dad starts making phone calls. This is the reason I never joined the police force and opted to go the PI route. Calling these things in, talking about them as if they're just procedure and not what they really are: travesties. I can't deal with this part. My visions make me too close to the victims. Every. Single. One. I felt the man's rage as he talked to Will. I knew his intentions long before Will figured them out. I feel like I'm the one who plunged that knife into his eye socket. Like I'm the one who slit Will's Achilles tendon.

I double over and throw up in the grass.

CHAPTER SEVENTEEN

"Hey, do you want me to drive you home?" Mitchell asks, placing his hand on my lower back and moving me away from the car.

The place has become an absolute mad house. Now that it's the scene of a murder, Weltunkin Park is being roped off by police tape. It won't be long before the media shows up and Will's murder is all over the news.

"Piper?" Mitchell stops walking and stares at me. "Talk to me."

"I can't leave. We have to search these woods. Veronica is nearby. I can feel it." My eyes scan the trees in the distance. There used to be walking paths, but after a few incidents with hunters using them to kill bears, the paths were closed. Now the park is strictly the lake, picnic areas, and playground. The woods are off-limits. Not that that made a difference to the man who has Veronica.

"We have plenty of guys on the way to search this place. We're going to find her."

But I have to be there when we do. "The driving gloves

Will was wearing, they were a gift from Veronica." The words tumble from my lips without prompting.

Mitchell cocks his head. "You saw that?"

"No. I just know it's true. I think Veronica tried to buy that video back from Will. He has no money to his name, so she bought him things."

"That makes sense. No one who drives that piece of crap"—he motions to the beat-up Ford—"would wear leather driving gloves."

"I've been interpreting my visions incorrectly. I was focusing on Veronica, but Will was the key. I was supposed to save him, too." I look down at my shoes, which are soaked through by the wet grass. "I should've figured this out sooner."

"It's my fault, isn't it?" Mitchell says.

I raise my gaze to meet his.

"I forced my way onto this team. You and your dad were doing great before I came along. And now..."

"You think you disrupted my visions?"

"I saw the way you looked at me when I first witnessed a vision. You were guarded. What if that stopped you from truly seeing what you were supposed to?"

He has a point, and one I've contemplated before. Still, this isn't his fault. If anything, it's mine. "I've been having visions for sixteen years. They've never been perfect. It's not science. Nothing is concrete."

He puts his hands on his hips and exhales loudly. "I disagree. Everything you see, feel, hear...it's all true. It's all correct. Unlike our theories have been. You're the only sure thing on this case. We're making the rest up as we go."

I replay my visions in my mind, trying to piece together the puzzle.

The woods.

The opening where sunlight came through.

The whispered voices.

"I've got it. He was on a phone. That's why I couldn't make out the voices in my vision. He was talking into a phone. The person on the other end was yelling, but I was hearing it through a phone that wasn't on speaker."

Mitchell removes his phone from his jacket pocket. "I'm looking up the trails. Trying to see if there were ever any rest areas or bathrooms or anything along them."

Somewhere Veronica could be holed up. But who was the person on the other end of the phone? Someone is calling the shots. And if they were yelling at the guy who killed Catton, then that might mean the man wasn't supposed to kill anyone. Yes. He was supposed to use Catton—frame him for Veronica's kidnapping.

"Piper!" Dad calls, raising his hand in the air and waving me over.

Mitchell eyes me briefly, and we walk back to Dad.

"Got it," Dad says and ends the call. "The Castells got another email from the kidnapper," he tells us. "Victor is forwarding it to me now." He opens his email on the phone, and Mitchell and I wait while he reads it. "Damn it!"

I grab the phone from his hand, and Mitchell leans in to read with me.

You weren't supposed to show the cops our private communication. Now look what you've done. Catton was just a warm-up. As punishment, I want my money by tonight. No exceptions. Do not respond to this email. Do not go to the police. If you do, Veronica is dead.

"Why would he send this?" Mitchell asks. "Does the douche really care about his money more than his daughter?"

I hand the phone back to Dad. "He can't transfer that much money at once," I say.

"Castell said he transferred the maximum amount allowed. He's hoping that will appease the kidnapper until we can find Veronica." Dad huffs. "We have a matter of hours to comb these woods and get her to safety. That's exactly what he's counting on us to do."

We're searching for a man we don't know. I'm the only one who's seen him, and I can't give the police much to go on. I need another vision. I need more. I grab my hair in frustration.

"What's up?" Mitchell asks me.

"I need to look for more clues. Go on ahead. You don't need me wandering these woods with you right now."

"Piper, you searching the woods is our best bet," Dad says. "You'll recognize the area from your vision."

"No. I saw the beginning of one of the paths. That's it. I need another vision to see more." Only I don't know what to look for to trigger that vision. The car again? Or... "Oh God." My stomach lurches.

"What's...?" Mitchell follows my gaze, which is trained on the trunk of the car. The coroner is on site now, getting ready to bag up the body.

"Wait!" I yell. "Don't move him." I rush over, though every fiber of my being is telling me not to do this. I've never read a dead body before. I've never even touched one. Not once in my life.

"Piper, are you sure about this?" Mitchell keeps in step with me, stopping next to me when we reach the trunk.

"I don't have a choice, do I? We have hours. That's it." A light rain begins to fall. All this rain is washing away evidence. Washing away footprints, blood, and all traces of

Veronica. But it can't wash away my visions. They're all we have left to go on.

"What can I do?" Mitchell asks me.

"You're doing it." I give him a small smile. He really has changed since we started this case. Dare I say we're actually friends at this point?

He nods, knowing his presence alone is a big help. I move toward Will's body, trying not to look at his face. I decide to touch his hand, which is still covered with the leather gloves—the gloves Veronica gave him. Yes, they're connected to her, so they're my best bet. Mitchell sees my intention and gently tilts Will's body so I can get to the gloves.

"Whatever you see, I'm right here." His green eyes convey so much warmth.

I inhale deeply and lay my hand on top of Will's.

"Where are we? Why are you doing this to me, Will?" Veronica is crying, huddled in the corner of a dark, wooden room. The rain sounds on the roof.

"Why? You refused to listen to me. I gave you every opportunity, and you just wouldn't listen, you stupid bitch." Will stands over her, a needle in his hand.

"What is that? What are you going to do?" she pleads with him.

"This?" He holds up the needle. "You know what this is. This is the magic juice I used on you that night. The one that made you listen to everything I said. I was hoping I wouldn't need it anymore, but you've made that decision for me."

"Please. I'll listen. I'll do whatever you say. I'll go back to the school with you. Just untie me."

Will bends down so he's eye level with Veronica. "You think I'm stupid? You ran away from me once already. You blew your chance."

"I won't do it again. I'm sorry. I'm so sorry. Will, please. I thought we had something."

He laughs in her face. "You thought wrong. You know what spoiled little rich girls are good for?"

Tears stream down her cheeks and dot her pants, which are caked in mud.

"They're good for two things: money and stripping." He laughs. "Sure, you entertained my frat buddies and paid for our parties. But I'm getting tired of your antics. Tired of having to tell you twice. So I'm not going to do that anymore." He holds up the needle. "You see, I'm sort of a genius. My IQ is off the charts. I created this drug." He nods. "Yes, that's right. You're my little test monkey. How does it feel to know you're helping science? This drug is a little like the date rape drug. You won't remember anything, and you'll pretty much do anything I ask you to. The difference is that it gets injected instead of ingested."

"Please don't. You don't need that. I promise."

"What? You're going to be a good little girl? Is that what you're saying?"

"Yes!" She nods, but cringes when her head feels like it's going to explode. "Please. My head hurts so much."

"A concussion will do that." He brushes her hair aside. "You've got a nasty bruise from that horse."

She leans into his hand. "Will, remember last weekend? We were happy together."

He laughs. "You really think I have feelings for you? I knew who you were when you showed up at that party. I knew you had money. My dad might be a janitor, but I have bigger aspirations. Your dad's money funds so many projects. Medical projects. I know all about them. I intend to follow in your dad's footsteps. Only I'm going to be more involved than he is. I believe in earning your paychecks." He shrugs.

"Maybe my stepdad taught me that. Or maybe I just like experimenting." He flicks the needle with his finger. "It is fun."

"No." The word is more sob than speech.

"The good news is you won't feel pain after I inject you with this. So you see, I'm helping you." He brushes her hair off her neck again. "You should thank me."

"I guess I should." The voice comes from behind Will, who whips around and stares at the entrance to the barn.

"Who the hell are you?" Will stands up, needle at the ready.

The bearded man smirks. "I'm the one who is going to benefit from this one's millions."

Will's face turns bright red, and he advances on the man, the needle held out, ready to plunge into the man. But he's too strong for Will. He lands a right hook to Will's jaw and wrestles the needle from his hand. The second he has it, he jabs Will in the neck with it before he can fully recover from the punch. Will's eyes widen, and then his body goes slack.

"Well, what do we have here?" the man asks. "Got to hand it to ya, kid. This stuff, whatever the hell it is, is pure gold for my needs." He motions to the corner of the barn beside Veronica. "Go sit down with her."

Will turns and does what the man asks.

"Who are you?" Veronica cowers, clearly not wanting to be near Will or this man.

"I'm your new best friend for the next few days. We're going to have ourselves a little adventure, and if you're good, you'll get to go back to your cushy little lifestyle, though you'll do it without your money. Still, you'll have your house. You may have to sell your horses, but after the way that one kicked you in the head, I doubt you'll mind getting rid of him."

"You've been following me?"

He nods. "For a while now. I've been watching every-thing you do. And that one right there"—he points to Will —"he's going to go down for kidnapping you. You got that? If you ever tell anyone about me, I'm going to come back." He moves toward Veronica. "And I'm going to see to it that you never get to take another breath." He grips her throat tightly in his hands, squeezing so hard she can't even gasp. "I'll end you for good. Forget about fancy drugs. You'll wish this one was still jerking you around like his little play thing. Do you understand?"

Fingers wrap around mine, and I open my eyes to see Mitchell staring back at me. "Relax. Just breathe."

My chest heaves, and I gulp in air. My free hand goes to my throat where I can still feel the pressure of the man's hand on Veronica's neck. "The barn. He was holding her in the barn."

"Who? Will?"

I nod. "But then the bearded man showed up. He drugged Will, too. Not just Veronica. He was planning to frame Will for Veronica's kidnapping. He's after her money. He's been watching her for a while." I know the question Mitchell's going to ask next. "I don't know who he is. No name or how he's connected to the Castells. But he seemed to know a lot about her."

"Because he was following her?"

I shrug. "I'm not sure. I think we should go to the barn, though. There might be something there to give me another clue." The vision was longer than usual. It was like watching a movie instead of only seeing glimpses. That means I'm getting closer to figuring this out. Things are making more sense.

Dad comes over to Mitchell and me. "I'm heading in

there with the others." His gaze falls on my hand, which is still in Mitchell's. "You two coming?"

"No. I need to go back to the Castells'. I think there's a clue there that I'm missing. We'll call you if we find anything that might lead you to where Veronica is."

Dad nods and jogs off to meet the other officers and the dogs waiting at the entrance to the old paths in the woods.

"You ready?" Mitchell asks, giving my hand a squeeze.

"Yeah, let's do this."

CHAPTER EIGHTEEN

According to procedure, Mitchell and I should go to the house first and let the Castells know we need to search the barn, but I don't have time for procedure right now. Nor do I give a damn if Victor or Darla presses charges for me searching without a warrant. The gate at the top of the road is open, which means Terry is most likely here taking care of the horses.

Mitchell pulls his Explorer through the gate and down to the stables. Sure enough, Terry is brushing Maggie when we pull up. He squints at the SUV. It's stopped raining, and the sun is trying to peak through the clouds. I step out of the vehicle and give him a wave.

"Hi, Terry. Do you remember me?"

He wipes his sleeve across his forehead. "Ms. Ashwell, right?"

"Yes. This is Detective Brennan." I motion to Mitchell. "Detective, this is Terrance Walsh. He tends to the horses."

Mitchell holds out a hand to Terry, who shakes it and then resumes brushing Maggie.

"What can I do for you both? Mrs. Castell didn't inform me you were stopping by." The meaning behind his words is clear.

"Unfortunately, time isn't our friend today, Terry. I need to see the barn. We believe Veronica was held there briefly after being kidnapped."

"In my barn?" He shakes his head. "I don't think so. Nothing was out of the ordinary. I would have noticed." He stops brushing the horse and looks up at Mitchell and me. "You don't think I—?"

I hold up a hand to stop him. "No, Terry. We don't. I think this happened late at night, after you had already gone for the day. We're looking for a bearded man in his fifties. Have you seen anyone fitting that description around here before?"

"Bearded, you say?"

I step toward him. "Yes. You've seen him, haven't you?"

He looks down at the brush in his hand. "I'm not sure. I was up at the house a few weeks ago, and there was a man getting into his car. He might have had a beard. It was early in the morning. I had to be here for a vet appointment. One of the horses had some issues during the night. I suspected it was a twisted gut. I had to call the vet to come in right away. We were afraid Penny Lane wouldn't make it through the day. She had to have surgery, so naturally I needed the Castells to sign off on it." He wipes his forehead again. "I thought it was odd that they had company so early in the morning. At least, company of that gender."

"What does that mean?" Mitchell asks, jotting this down on his notepad.

Terry's eyes widen. "I shouldn't have said that."

I move toward him, bending down so I'm at his level on the small stool. "Terry, anything you know might help us find Veronica. If we don't get to her today, she will die. Now, you might not see how this detail could be related to her kidnapping, but there's a good chance we will. Please."

He swallows so hard I hear it. "Well, Mr. Castell has been known to have women come to the house from time to time."

Victor Castell openly has affairs in his own home? "Does Mrs. Castell know about this?" I ask him, trying to keep my voice level.

Terry nods. "They have separate bedrooms for a reason. Their marriage is just for show. Mrs. Castell stays around for the money."

For the money, not for their daughter? What is it with these people? They all love their cash more than their flesh and blood.

"How long have you worked for the Castells?" Mitchell asks, his pen poised and ready.

"Twelve years now."

"So, you'd say you know them pretty well?" Mitchell scribbles on his pad, but his eyes remain focused on Terry. I know he's trying to read Terry's expression to determine if he's being completely honest.

"As well as anyone can ever know an employer. We don't cross paths much, to be honest. I come here, tend to the horses, and only go to the house when there's an emergency."

"How many times would you say you've been inside the house?" I ask.

"To date, only a handful."

A handful of times in twelve years. That's not much to go on.

"Do you think this man you saw, the one who might

have had a beard, could have been visiting Mrs. Castell?" Mitchell quirks an eyebrow.

Terry holds up his hands, waving them in front of him. "I'm not one to gossip about who might be having an affair. I shouldn't have told you about Mr. Castell as it is."

"You do know that we're asking these questions as part of an ongoing police investigation and that not answering to the best of your abilities could be seen as withholding information from the authorities." Mitchell stands up taller, clearly trying to intimidate Terry. Part of me wants to step in on Terry's behalf, but we need answers now.

Terry meets my gaze as if he's waiting for me to come to his aid as well. I simply nod for him to tell us what he knows. "I see. Well, I've never seen any men go to the house to visit Mrs. Castell, but like I said, their marriage isn't exactly on the up-and-up, so I wouldn't be surprised if she's seeing other people on the side like he is."

"Thank you, Terry," I say. "We'll let you get back to work here." I gesture to the horse.

"Ms. Ashwell," Terry says as I start for the Explorer.

"Yes?" I answer, meeting his gaze.

"Something's off about that family. You see all these horses?"

I nod.

"They all belong to Veronica. Every single one of them. What does one girl need with four horses? Especially when she barely spends any time at home."

"What do you mean?" Mitchell asks. "Where was she before college?"

"Boarding school. She came home for holidays and birthdays. That was all. And sometimes when I'm leaving at night, I see lights on in all three upstairs bedrooms, the ones with the balconies. Why use three rooms?"

Because Mr. Castell is having affairs. They don't even share a bedroom. And that explains why Veronica has so few personal effects in her room. She never really lived there. That entire house is for show, just like the rest of their lives.

"Thank you again, Terry. You've been very helpful," I say. "We really do need to check the barn."

Terry shakes his head. "I'm sorry, Ms. Ashwell. You seem like a nice lady, but this is private property, and if you don't have the Castells' permission to search the barn"—he looks at Mitchell—"or a search warrant, then I'm afraid I can't let you do that. I'm not about to lose my job over this."

"Want me to put in a call for a warrant?" Mitchell asks.

"No." I start toward the Explorer. "Let's go talk to the Castells. It will be quicker."

"So it's a marriage for show, right?" Mitchell says once he's behind the wheel and driving us up to the entrance.

"Seems that way."

"Think they actually slept together to conceive Veronica, or do you think Darla was artificially inseminated with Victor's sperm?"

I cringe. "Ugh, I'd rather not contemplate things like that. The potential visuals that accompany such thoughts are too much for me to bear."

"What's the plan? Are you going to tell them what you saw in your vision and that you need to search the barn?"

"Direct does seem to be the best approach, but I think there's more we aren't seeing here." I run through Terry's words in my head. "It's possible Terry didn't see the exact man we're looking for leaving the Castells' house, but what if he did?"

"Then that means the kidnapper knows the Castells, which is pretty typical. It would have to be someone who knows about Castell's money at the very least." Mitchell pulls up the driveway and parks, but instead of getting out, he turns in his seat so he's facing me. "It could be a business partner or a business rival. Or it could be one of Darla's lovers."

"One of? You think she has multiple lovers on the side?"

He shrugs. "Sounds like Victor does, so why not her, too?"

"You've seen her, right?"

"Tell me you wouldn't sleep with someone who was loaded and could buy you whatever pretty things you wanted."

"I wouldn't. That's disgusting. Would you?"

He looks up at the roof of the Explorer, like he's contemplating it.

I smack his arm. "Clearly I've given you too much credit these past few days." I start to get out of the car, but he grabs my arm.

"I was teasing you, Piper. Loosen up a little. I find with our line of work, you need to laugh whenever possible because the gravity of what we do can drown you."

He's right. I laugh about the littlest things because if I didn't, I'd curl up in a ball and rock myself to sleep every night from all the horrors I've seen. This is a rewarding profession, but getting to the point of rescuing a missing person can be pure hell. William Catton's butchered eye flashes in my mind. As awful as Catton was, I didn't want to see him murdered. I wanted him behind bars, serving time for his crimes. Now all I can do is find this bearded man and make sure he never sees the light of day from outside the walls of a prison.

Mitchell removes his hand from my arm. "You weren't reading me somehow were you?"

I hold up my right hand. "Not without using this. You're completely safe."

"So I can touch you, but you can't touch me. Got it." His cheeks redden. "I didn't mean for it to come out that way."

"Let's go, Romeo. We have a case to solve, and we're losing daylight." Considering how early we got up, the day is flying by. I open the car door and step out. My eyes go to the three balconies, and I see the curtain move in the middle bedroom. Someone knows we're here.

We walk up to the door, and Mitchell rings the bell. To my surprise, it's Mrs. Castell who answers the door.

"Did I somehow miss your phone call?" she asks, no warmth in her voice.

"Is your husband home?" I ask, leaving off the rest of my question: or is he out with one of his mistresses?

"No, he had a business meeting he couldn't get out of. What is it you need?" She stands squarely in the doorway, blocking our entry.

"Mrs. Castell, do you know a man in his fifties with a graying beard?"

"That's a rather vague description, don't you think?"

I don't want to throw Terry under the bus here, but I don't know how else to make her talk. "I had a vision of this man. I believe he took Veronica. We were just down by the horse stables, and Terry—"

"Who's Terry?" she asks.

"The man who takes care of your horses." Is she really that stuck up that she doesn't know the names of the people she employs?

"They are not *my* horses. They're Veronica's. I have nothing to do with them."

"Mr. Walsh..." Mitchell pauses at the look of confusion

on Darla's face. "That's Terry's last name," he clarifies. "He told us he had to come up to the house a few weeks ago because one of the horses was having a problem and needed medical attention. He believes he saw this man leaving the house."

"Then he must be a business associate of Victor's. You'll have to ask him when he gets home." She starts to close the door, but I put my hand on it to stop her. She fights me, pushing back against the door, and I decide to take drastic measures. Her diamond tennis bracelet dangles from her arm, and I reach for it, letting my index finger loop through it.

"You are not writing her another check. That would be the second one this month! She has her own account for God's sake." Darla grabs the checkbook in Victor's hand.

"This was the arrangement for her silence."

"Let go of me!" Darla yells, tugging the bracelet out of my grasp.

"What did you see?" Mitchell asks me.

"How dare you? I insist you arrest her!" Darla clutches her bracelet to her chest. "She tried to steal my jewelry right off my wrist. You saw her!"

Mitchell holds up a hand. "Mrs. Castell, you need to calm down. You and I both know that's not at all what Ms. Ashwell was doing." Darla starts to shut the door again, but Mitchell sticks his foot in the way and forces the door back open with his palm. "Mrs. Castell, it would not be in your best interest to do anything to stymie this investigation. It's your daughter's life at stake. You're well aware of Piper's abilities, and I think it's pretty clear she just had a vision while touching your bracelet."

The garage door closest to us opens, and Victor's BMW

pulls into it. But instead of the door closing, Victor walks out and comes over to us. "What's going on here?"

"Something I'm willing to bet is very much illegal," Darla says, clutching her bracelet once again. "This woman tried to take my diamonds."

Instead of responding to Darla's accusation, I turn to Victor. "Whose silence are you paying for?"

CHAPTER NINETEEN

"I assure you I don't know what you're talking about." Victor pushes past us into the house.

Darla tries to get to the door before we barge inside, but she's too slow. "I'm calling the police!"

"No need. I'm already here," Mitchell says, flashing his badge. "I can't believe you'd make us go through the time it would take to procure a search warrant when it's your daughter's life on the line. You've both read the latest email from the kidnapper. We're running out of time, and Piper— Ms. Ashwell is very close to finding Veronica."

Victor turns to look at me. "You are? Do you know where she is? Who took her? I was just at the bank. Should I stop the next transfer of money?"

"Do either one of you truly love your daughter? I'm really trying to figure you out, but you both seem so obsessed with your money. So much so that you're willing to risk Veronica's safety."

"She's with a kidnapper. She's not safe!" Darla yells, her foot on the bottom stair, ready to flee up the staircase at a moment's notice.

"Retreating to your bedroom already?" I ask her. "Tell me, how long have you and your husband been occupying separate rooms?"

Her nostrils flare, and she grips the banister so tightly her knuckles whiten. "Our relationship is none of your business."

"How long have you two been separated?" Mitchell asks.

"We're still legally married. We share a house, a family, everything but bedrooms." Victor's voice is stoic, totally void of feeling, which I suppose is appropriate since he harbors no feelings for his wife. But clearly she's a different story. It's written all over her face. She loved him once. What changed? What happened to make her tolerate this arrangement?

"You know he's having affairs, don't you?" I ask, moving toward her. "You must have seen the women leaving the house."

She takes two steps up the stairs, keeping distance between us after I read her without her permission earlier. "Of course. I'm not an idiot."

"So what? He pays you for your silence so you don't smear his name to the public? Why not simply divorce?" I cock my head at her, trying to figure out where her dignity is. Or does she still love him despite what he's doing?

Victor laughs. "Divorce? Darla wouldn't hear of it." He holds out his hand, motioning the length of her body. "All she knows how to be is my wife, and she's good at that, in public at least."

Mitchell leans toward me and whispers, "But clearly not in the bedroom."

Is that what this is about? Darla doesn't put out, so

Victor finds women who will. "So you have an agreement?" I ask.

Darla nods. "What do I care what he does? It doesn't affect me. In fact, it gives me some peace and quiet."

These people are more messed up than I ever thought. They're putting on all these airs, pretending to care about their daughter's disappearance when it's clear to me that they care about their money more.

Money. That's why Darla is staying with him. He's paying her to. I turn to Victor. "You don't want her to divorce you either, because it would make you look bad if the truth about your affairs came to light." But in my vision he was paying someone else. Not Darla. "Who else knows? Someone does, and you're paying her to keep quiet."

Victor turns and walks into his study. The rest of us follow. Even Darla, to my surprise. He sits down at his desk and opens a drawer. "I've paid too many people over the years, which is how news about my money has spread. I'm a silent partner in many businesses. My name is supposed to stay out of everything. I fund projects, and I make billions because of it. But I suppose I can't keep something like this from you, Ms. Ashwell. I never would have gone to your father if I knew he would put you on the case. And I certainly tried my best to keep you away from anything that would lead you to discovering this truth."

I move closer, examining the small safe he's removing from the desk drawer. He takes a key from the pocket of his black dress pants and opens the safe. Retrieving an envelope, he sighs and stares at me before saying, "You can never reveal what I'm about to show you."

"Ms. Ashwell can't promise that without knowing the contents," Mitchell says.

"Victor," Darla says in a hushed voice. "Don't. You'll

ruin everything. Years of hard work. Don't do this," she pleads.

Now I need to know what's in that envelope. I reach my hand out, hoping to touch it before he can second-guess himself.

"Don't let her touch it!" Darla shrieks.

Before she can stop him, Victor shoves the envelope in my hands.

"You will list Darla Castell as the birth mother," Victor says, his finger stabbing the birth certificate on the desk in front of him.

The man sitting at the desk is wearing a white doctor's coat. He's small with thin wire glasses. "Mr. Castell, I can't do that. You're asking me to forge a legal document. I could lose my license." He shakes his head. "I won't do it."

"You seem like a reasonable man, Dr. Ellery. You're young. I'm guessing early thirties. Imagine a life on the beach somewhere with a beautiful woman by your side. You won't need to work another day in your life if you do this. I'll keep paying your paycheck and then some, and you can retire now. Live the dream." Victor bends down. "The birth mother is on board already. She doesn't want this child. My wife and I do. You see, Darla can't have children, which just isn't acceptable. I need an heir, and this child is in fact mine. I'm her biological father."

Mitchell is restraining Darla when the vision fades. Tears are streaming down her cheeks, taking her black mascara and foundation with it. "You bastard!" she screams at Victor. "How could you do this to me? I loved you, but that wasn't enough. I couldn't give you a child, and you've held it against me time and time again."

Mitchell looks over Darla's head at me since he's the

only one who hasn't been clued in on the truth surrounding Veronica's birth.

"She's not your daughter," I say, addressing Darla. I turn my head to see Victor, who is standing at the window, peering out at the darkening sky. The clouds that have rolled in are making it unusually dark for late afternoon. "You had an affair and got another woman pregnant."

"He did it on purpose. I know he did. And then he bought his own child from that woman. He kept paying her, all these years, to keep her fat trap closed."

"Who is she? Is it possible she had Veronica kidnapped?" I ask.

Victor whirls around. "Becky would never do that. She wanted Veronica, but her husband wouldn't hear of it. You see Ed and Darla have something in common. Neither of them are capable of having children. He knew the child wasn't his, so he sent Becky away when she reached her second trimester and started showing."

"No one knew she was pregnant," I say. "That doctor, Doctor Ellery, he had a British accent. You and Ed sent Becky to England to have her baby, didn't you?"

Victor nods. "We were sparing two families from shame. Becky agreed it was for the best."

"Let me get this straight," Mitchell says. "You and this guy Ed are both married to women you're only pretending to be in love with, and really you are Becky's lover?"

"Becky and I are long over," Victor says. "She was taking all my money, so I threatened to go to the media and tell the truth."

"She knew you wouldn't because you'd be implicating yourself!" Darla says. "Ed and I are the victims here. We're the ones who suffered because of you two."

"You're both reaping the benefits, though," Mitchell

says. "You're both getting money in exchange for keeping up this ruse."

"Does Becky know her daughter is missing?" I ask.

Darla starts laughing. "Becky doesn't care about Veronica. She never has. If she did, she never would have agreed to Victor's plan in the first place. She doesn't call to check up on her. She doesn't ask for pictures. Nothing. She does call and email for money, though. That's for sure."

Poor Veronica. Her own mother gave her up, and she wound up stuck with Darla, who might be even worse.

"Are you thinking Becky is the one who took Veronica?" Victor asks. "She's a little unhinged after everything, but I don't see her doing something like this."

"Yeah, she has no reason to since you give her and Veronica all your money anyway." Something about Darla's comment gives me pause. She might have loved her husband once, but that feeling has been replaced with bitterness and distrust. I can't blame her since he had an affair, but she's the one who chose to stay with him. No one forced her.

"We're going to have to talk to Becky and her husband," Mitchell says. He meets my eyes. "I'm calling your father to get him up to speed." He steps out of the room, leaving me with Victor and Darla, neither of whom will look at each other or me.

"Mr. and Mrs. Castell, I know this is a very personal question, but we don't have time for privacy right now. I need to know who else knew about this arrangement. Other than Doctor Ellery"—whom I have no idea how to track down since he lives in England—"and of course Becky and Ed."

"No one," Victor says. "We were extremely careful." Victor walks over to a photograph on the bookshelf. He picks it up and hands it to me. "Veronica looks like me instead of her mother. That always worked in our favor. People just assumed my genetic traits were the dominant ones. It's not uncommon."

No, it's not, which is why I never questioned it. Veronica has her father's features. If she'd had Becky's, this plan wouldn't have gone so smoothly. I stare at the photograph, which couldn't look more staged. Darla's smile is completely forced. My guess is she doesn't like being this close to her pretend family. Yet a few days ago she seemed at ease putting her arm around her husband. What was the difference? Was Victor making Darla uncomfortable, or was it Veronica?

I turn around to look at Darla, who is edging her way out of the room. "Mrs. Castell?"

"What now? Shouldn't you be out looking for Veronica? Your deadline is almost up and yet here you stand, questioning us about things that have absolutely nothing to do with who took our daughter."

"Except she's not *your* daughter. You've never thought about her that way, have you?" I turn the photograph around for her to see. "Even though you couldn't have a child, and some would think you'd be happy at the idea of getting to raise one, you couldn't look at Veronica without seeing Becky, could you?"

"You're wrong, Ms. Ashwell," Victor says. "We are well past that. While our relationship might be more business arrangement than anything else now, Darla does not harbor ill feelings toward Veronica. That's simply absurd."

"Is it?" I keep my gaze on Darla, who continues to back out of the room. I follow her, and in order to watch me, she's forced to walk backward. She nearly stumbles when her foot hits the bottom step of the staircase. I reach for her, my only intention to keep her from falling, but something much better happens.

"How long do you expect to keep going on like this?" Darla says, pulling her robe around her body. She stands in front of the balcony doors, holding the white curtains aside to peer out. "Neither one of them realizes that we are the ones cleaning up their messes. Us." She lets go of the curtain as a blue sedan pulls into the driveway. She whirls around on a man with a graying beard and a round nose. "You need to leave. The stable hand is on his way inside. If he finds you with me..."

"If he asks, I'll say I had an early business meeting with Victor. Just keep the man out of the house." The man heads for the door without another word.

"Get off of me!" Darla is swatting at my back, and I realize we're in a heap at the bottom of the stairs. "Get her off now!"

Mitchell pulls me to my feet, holding me by my shoulders and looking into my eyes. "You saw something, didn't you?"

"Not much, but enough all the same." My eyes go to Darla. "It's Ed. He's the bearded man who killed William Catton and kidnapped Veronica."

"Ed Haynes?" Victor asks, his brow furrowing.

Darla fixes her hair, which is sticking out on both sides, and then pats down the front of her pants suit. "I wouldn't know anything about what that wretched man did or didn't do."

Darla's earlier comment comes to mind. "You said before that you and Ed were the real victims."

"Tom," Mitchell says into his phone, and it registers as strange that he and Dad are on a first name basis. "The man we're looking for is one Edward Haynes."

"This is completely absurd," Darla says, backing up the stairs.

"Mrs. Castell, I need to see your bedroom," I tell her.

"Absolutely not!" she shrieks. "This is my house, and you have no right to search my belongings for anything." She looks over my head. "Victor, do something. Make her leave. You can't let her accuse me of having anything to do with Veronica's disappearance."

"I never accused you of anything, Mrs. Castell." I keep my voice completely calm even though I want to storm up these steps and barge into her room. "I simply had a vision of Edward Haynes in your bedroom, and I'd like to see your room in hopes of finding him."

"Darla," Victor says, confusion filling his tone. "What was Ed doing in this house? We both agreed neither he nor Becky were permitted to step foot on this property."

In my vision, Darla was wearing a robe. That could mean... "You're having an affair with him, aren't you?" What better revenge than sleeping with her husband's mistress's husband?

Victor steps past me up the stairs. "Is this true? Are you and Ed...?" For someone who is no stranger to infidelity, he's sure taking this pretty hard. "Did you know he kidnapped Veronica? Did you two...plan this?" His voice cracks. Maybe he does have some paternal instincts after all.

"I'm not going to stand here and listen to this from you of all people." She reaches out and slaps him across the face. She attempts to do it again, but he grabs her wrist.

"Ms. Ashwell," Victor says, his eyes still glued to his wife. "You have my permission to search anywhere you'd like in this house."

"No!" Darla shrieks.

"Thank you," I say, rushing up the stairs.

Darla reaches out, grabbing me by my hair. She yanks me backward, and we both almost topple down the stairs. But Victor grabs his wife around her waist, and Mitchell rushes to my aid.

"I'm fine," I tell him. While Darla is restrained, I reach for her wrist. She tries to fight me, but Victor pins her arms down. He's not hurting her, so I decide to look the other way and not try to stop the domestic dispute in the making. I close my fingers around the diamond tennis bracelet again.

"She said she's going for a ride before she leaves. If you head down to the stables now, you'll be able to stop her." Darla stands in front of her bedroom mirror, removing her jewelry from the day while carefully balancing her phone between her ear and shoulder.

"I'm on it. Get to work on the ransom note. I don't want to give Becky any more time to get money out of Victor. She's got a separate bank account. I'm not getting any of that money." He practically growls into the phone.

Darla removes her tennis bracelet. "Don't worry. As long as you stick to the plan and don't let Veronica see your face, we'll both be billionaires in a matter of days."

I let go of the bracelet and step back. "It was all your idea, wasn't it? You came up with the plan and made Ed do your dirty work. You probably only slept with him to convince him to kidnap Veronica and keep your hands clean so to speak."

"Why would you do this?" Victor's grip tightens on his wife.

Mitchell reaches for Darla. "Mr. Castell, you need to take your hands off her."

Victor lets go, and Darla rubs her arms where he held her. "I should press charges for that. How dare you?" she lashes out at him.

"Enough!" I say, ready to be finished with the entire Castell family. The more I learn about them, the more I realize they're all completely screwed up. "Mrs. Castell, you'd better start talking." What she should do is insist on a lawyer, but if she does, it will take too long to get the answers I need. "Did you plan this kidnapping with Ed Haynes?"

"I merely planted the idea in Ed's head. It didn't take much convincing. He did all the work, though. You can't arrest me for an idea."

"Actually, I can," Mitchell says. "You helped plan a kidnapping. That's a crime."

"She's wasting away thousands each semester at that college, and she's barely passing her classes. All she does is drink and party, expecting Victor and I to write checks and donate money so she can keep up the pretense of being intelligent. She's intelligent all right. She's a conniving thief! She doesn't deserve any of that money. I'm the one who has to put up with that man day in and day out. Me!" She jabs a finger at her chest. "I lie for him and put on a smile, and what does it get me?"

"How about a huge house and all the fancy jewelry you want?" Mitchell says, motioning around us.

Her face contorts in a look of pure disgust. "You think diamond bracelets make up for years of affairs?"

"Yeah, well now it looks like a nice pair of handcuffs is all you're going to get." He steps toward her, his cuffs in hand. He turns her around, brings her hands behind her back, and clamps the cuffs around her wrists. "Mrs. Castell, you have the right to remain silent..." He continues reading her rights, and man do I wish he'd stop. I need to ask her more questions.

In the meantime, I run over the entire case in my mind.

She planned this, which means she must know where Ed took Veronica. "Where did he bring her? We found Will Catton's car in Lake Harmon. Veronica's blood was at the scene as well. Is he in the woods at the park?" Please say yes. That would mean our guys are well on their way to finding her.

"I'm not talking without my lawyer present," Darla says.

Victor's jaw sets. "You're going to need to hire one, seeing as the one you typically use is my lawyer and I'll be using him to help me prosecute you."

Darla looks like she wants to spit in his face, and then her breathing gets erratic. She's having a panic attack.

"Where is her medication?" Mitchell asks Victor.

"She's faking. She hasn't had an actual panic attack in years." He waves a hand in her direction, dismissing her act.

Her last supposed panic attack occurred when we were emailing the kidnapper. "You left the room when the emails from the kidnapper came in. Were they from you?"

"Did you expect Ed to email from the woods? He's barely getting cell reception. Our phone calls have all been interrupted." I guess she figures since her lawyer won't be of any help she might as well take credit for what she's done.

"So you faked a panic attack to go send those emails?"

She smiles at me. "You thought you were so clever with your little freakish abilities." She juts her chin out at me. "But look at what I was able to do right underneath your nose."

"Where is she?" I yell, gripping the banister to keep from ringing her neck and forcing Mitchell to arrest me for assault.

"I don't know!"

"Bullshit!" I move toward her, but Mitchell steps between us.

"Piper, calm down." His eyes convey what he can't communicate out loud: I'll get nothing out of her if I beat her until she's unconscious.

I decide to try a different approach. "Mrs. Castell, you're in a lot of trouble here, and if you don't want to spend life behind bars, I suggest you cooperate with us and help us find Veronica." I'm making false promises, but usually even criminals get a little consideration for cooperating with an investigation like this.

She looks to Victor, who nods. Their relationship will never make an iota of sense to me, but his reassurance does the trick.

"After Victor wired the money, Ed took off. He hasn't contacted me since, and he won't answer any of my phone calls. I have no idea where he took Veronica. Once you came onto the case, I told him not to tell me anything specific so you wouldn't be able to get anything out of me."

She's smart for doing that. All along I'd just pegged her as the cynic who didn't trust I could find her daughter. "Where did he take her initially?"

"He was supposed to hold her in the old barn on the outskirts of the property. It's falling down, and no one's used it in over a decade." She shrugs. "We never intended to hurt Veronica. We were only after the money. Ed was supposed to wear a ski mask so she couldn't identify him. Not that she would have known who he was since she'd never seen his face before. Or her mother's." She rolls her eyes, and for once I agree with her. It's crazy that Veronica's mother never wanted to see her. Never thought to get to know Veronica as someone other than her mother. A family friend, a fellow country club member, a distant cousin... There were so many possibilities.

"Anyway, she wouldn't be able to describe him to the

police. He was going to talk in a lower voice and everything." She tilts her head toward the step, indicating she'd like to sit down. Mitchell holds her arm as she lowers herself. "But that Will Catton showed up. Veronica did tell me about him. What he'd done to her. I pretended to care, but inside I figured it was karma. She was getting screwed over by the universe for being such an entitled brat. Served her right. And when Ed said Catton knocked her out with some drug, I thought the universe was finally smiling down on me. Helping me out. We'd frame Catton, who already had this kidnapping plan underway."

"But things took a turn for the worse, didn't they?" I ask, already knowing what happened.

"Catton was too smart. Ed had no choice but to take care of him. It was self-defense if you ask me. Catton had the means to kill Ed with those drugs he made."

A rather twisted take on the real events, but I'm not about to defend Catton either.

"My guess is that Ed took Veronica into those woods somewhere and got greedy."

"Or he was afraid you'd double-cross him," Mitchell says.

"That too." She chuckles. "Maybe he isn't as dumb as I thought."

"What now?" Victor asks.

"Now, we take a field trip to Darla's room and I try my damnedest to find Veronica before Ed does something really stupid."

CHAPTER TWENTY

This time Darla doesn't protest as I ascend the stairs to her bedroom. Thanks to my visions, I know my previous assumption about which room is hers was correct. I reach for the doorknob only to find it locked. I turn to Darla, who shrugs.

"Don't tell me you expected anything different," she says. "The key is in my pants pocket. Right side." She dips her head in the direction.

Mitchell removes her handcuffs, which I'm assuming is to persuade her to keep helping us. Maybe he can get her a deal if she can lead us to Veronica.

She grabs the key, inserts it, and opens the door. The room is gigantic. My entire apartment would fit inside it. I recognize the balcony and the vanity from my visions. Ed was standing in the center of the room when he was here. It's possible I'm right and they did share a bed before he left, but considering that was weeks ago, I doubt I'll get a read off Darla's sheets, nor do I want to. In the other vision, Darla was talking to Ed on the phone.

I turn around, noticing she's standing in front of the

vanity, looking at her reflection in the mirror. Is she envisioning herself in an orange prison jumpsuit?

"Mrs. Castell, I'd like to see your phone." I hold my hand out to her.

She nods and removes the phone from the drawer in her vanity. "This is the one I use to talk to Ed. He's the only one who has this number."

She used a separate phone. It's a cheap prepaid phone you can buy in a drug store. I should have noticed it in my vision, but she'd had it between her shoulder and ear, blocking it from my view. This is more evidence against her. This crime was premeditated. I take the phone without mentioning this. I put it to my ear, which is something I've never done before when having a vision. Yet somehow I know I need to. I hold a finger to my lips, indicating for everyone to be silent.

Whispers of wind through the trees. Almost howling, like all their leaves are lost. The ground crunches, but not with the sound of dead leaves. This is rock.

Then it goes quiet. No footsteps. Only wind. How is wind getting through the trees? Now more rocks. Sliding. Sliding across each other.

"Damn it!" Ed's voice is a loud whisper.

Whispers.

Nothing but whispers.

All around.

Whispers in the woods.

I lower the phone. Everyone's eyes are trained on me, wanting to know what it is that I've discovered. "It doesn't make sense. All I heard were faint whispers of sounds. I didn't see anything." I rub my forehead, beyond frustrated. "I couldn't even sense Veronica. I don't know if she's still with him or if I was seeing Ed on his own." He could have been trying to evade the police. They might be nearby, and he was being exceptionally quiet so they didn't hear him.

Mitchell closes the bedroom door, motioning for Victor and Darla to stay put, and walks toward me. He brings me to the edge of the bed and sits me down. He sits close so we can speak quietly without being overheard. "Your earlier visions were trying to warn you about Catton, not Veronica. Is it possible this one is trying to do the same? I mean, not about Catton, but maybe there's something else. Maybe that's why you aren't focusing on Veronica."

"Or it could mean she isn't alive. That's happened before. I stop seeing the victim when..." I let the thought trail off as my mind fills with images of those people. All the ones I lost.

"Stop." He places his hand on mine. "Take a few deep breaths and focus. You saw Ed, right?"

I shake my head. "I heard him. Only him. Well, him and the sounds around him. But they were so soft."

"You mean muffled? Maybe something happened to Ed. Maybe he's hurt and that's how things sound to him right now."

It's a good theory, but it's wrong. I can feel it. "No. My last thought before the vision ended was 'whispers in the woods.'"

"Excuse me," Victor says. "But what did you just say?" He steps toward me. "Whispers in the woods? Was that it?"

"Yes. Why?"

"You don't know?"

"Know what?" Now I'm really frustrated. What is he seeing that I'm not when I'm the one with the visions?

"That's the name of a song written about a campground I went to nearby when I was a boy. They've taken down all the cabins, and the camp's been closed for years. There was a bear attack."

A bear attack. Weltunkin Park. "Wait! Was that campground in the woods surrounding Weltunkin Park?"

He nods. "It was a few miles west of the park. But like I said, the place was torn down."

"All of it?" I ask, remembering the sound of rock on rock. "Where there any concrete structures there?"

Victor's brow furrows, and he looks up at the ceiling as if trying to recall a distant memory. "There was an electrical building. It was small, though. Really small."

"Too small to hold two people?" Mitchell asks.

"They'd have to be standing up to fit inside it," Victor says. "Why? You think that's where Ed took Veronica?"

I meet Mitchell's gaze. "Call Dad. Tell him where to go."

Mitchell tries Dad's cell, but he shakes his head. "No luck. There must not be any cell service where he is."

The woods surrounding Weltunkin Park are vast. We have no idea which direction Dad and the others went in either. My eyes flit to the clock on the nightstand. 7:34.

"We need to go. Now."

"What about her?" Mitchell asks me. "I can't leave her here. She's under arrest."

"We'll bring them both. There are plenty of officers all over that park. Someone can watch her while we go get Veronica."

He nods and motions for Victor and Darla to come with us. Mitchell handcuffs Darla again once she's in the back of his Explorer, which makes me feel better. The woman is clearly unhinged, and I wouldn't put it past her to try to make Mitchell crash just so she has a chance to escape.

Victor is sitting as far away from his wife as the back seat will allow.

I try Dad's cell again, but I know he's put it on silent to keep it from alerting Ed where he is if he does get close. I shoot him a quick text, hoping he might see that if he checks his phone and can't play a voice mail.

Piper: Ed has Veronica in an electrical building on the old campground.

"What was the name of the camp?" I ask Victor, lowering my visor and using the mirror to see him better.

"Whispering Pines. There's a string of pine trees that bordered the cabins."

Piper: Whispering Pines.

I don't expect to get a reply, so I put my phone away and watch the minutes tick by until Mitchell pulls into Weltunkin Park. We're greeted by an armed officer at the gate. Mitchell lowers his window and flashes his badge.

I hold up my PI license and then jerk a finger toward the back seat. "We have Victor and Darla Castell. Darla has admitted to helping Edward Haynes abduct Veronica Castell. Detective Brennan's placed her under arrest. We'll need someone to watch over her while we go after Ed."

"Pull up to Officer Andrews over there." He points to an officer about fifty feet in front of us. "He'll watch your vehicle and the passengers for you."

Mitchell nods and pulls forward, getting out and talking to Officer Andrews.

"Stay put," I tell the Castells, eyeing them each briefly before locking the car and running toward the woods to the west.

Mitchell is on my heels in seconds. "Let me guess. You're a runner," he says.

"I would say the same about you considering how quickly you caught me."

"I only have time to run when I'm not on crazy cases like this one. Of course, crazy cases do mean things like running in the woods." He elbows my arm, and we enter the pathway.

Victor said we had to go a few miles to find the campgrounds, so we push the pace, not talking to conserve energy. I get a cramp in my side from neglecting exercise. I'm not a runner like Mitchell thinks. I just have long legs for my size, so I can cover more ground. And I'm stick thin, which means I'm not hauling any extra weight. After this, I might have to consider hitting the gym a few days a week.

I can tell Mitchell is holding back for my sake, and it urges me to push on. I'm not letting my endurance be the reason we don't get to Veronica in time. The wind starts to whistle through the trees, and the ground beneath our feet is no longer dirt and grass. We're running on rock.

This is it. I hold my arm out to slow Mitchell. He looks at me and nods in understanding. We creep to a walk, searching in all directions and trying not to make a sound. The rain begins to fall again, and I say a silent prayer of thanks. The noise will cover up our footsteps, and it feels amazing on my heated face after running about three miles.

This area is like a wind tunnel. My jacket billows out in the back, filling with air and chilling my sweaty skin. We keep walking, but my eyes close and I'm not following the surroundings in front of me. Instead, I'm following a scene in my mind. My vision. We're approaching the place where Ed stabbed the back of Veronica's neck with another concoction Will had cooked up. I don't know how many needles Will had or if Ed now possessed them all. I didn't have time to check in with Dad or the coroner who examined Will's body. There's a good possibility that Ed is armed with his knife and a few needles. We have to be careful.

Mitchell's hand slips into mine, and he directs me around something. Without opening my eyes, I know it's the puddle I saw in my vision. The one Veronica fell into. That has to mean we're close. I stop and turn in all directions, finally scanning the scene around me. Ed wouldn't have wanted to carry her for long. But there's no electrical building around.

Voices up ahead draw my focus. Then flashlights come into view. Mitchell and I run to meet up with the other officers. No point in being quiet now that the others are making noise. They've found the electrical building. Dad meets my gaze as he reaches for the door on the building. He tugs, but it won't open.

Rock on rock. Rock on rock. Rock on rock.

I'm not even touching anything, but the sound from my vision is overwhelming. I press the heel of my hand to my temple and resist the urge to cry out. I look down at the ground, and suddenly, I know what I need to do. My foot brushes aside the rocks beneath my feet, and underneath is a concrete slab.

Not rock on rock. Rock on concrete. I bend down, frantically pushing the rocks aside. Mitchell falls to his knees beside me and helps without question. Dad continues to pry the door.

"There's something wedged under the door, stopping it from opening," Dad says.

For a brief moment, I stop what I'm doing and press my hand to the bottom of the door. The image of a tire wrench comes into view.

"He didn't toss the tire wrench in the lake. He used it to

wedge the door. He's inside." I turn around, and Mitchell lowers his body so he's lying down in front of the door.

"I see it," Mitchell says. "I need something to knock it out of the way."

Easier said than done. Ed is going to be holding it in place on the other side. The building is solid concrete, which makes firing a gun at it, or even threatening to, completely useless.

"We know you're in their, Ed," I say, pressing my face against the cool concrete. "Come out with your hands up. Make this easier on yourself."

He doesn't answer, which is actually smart since we can't arrest him if he doesn't come out. He's hoping we won't ever get inside. But he's an absolute idiot for thinking we'd just leave without him. That leaves him with two options: surrender and face prison or die inside there. Right now, I'm not sure which one I'm rooting for because I'm positive Veronica isn't inside there with him.

I lower myself in front of the concrete slab on the ground again and finish clearing it of rocks.

"What are you doing? I thought you were just clearing it so we could see what was jammed under the door."

I shake my head. "Veronica is under here."

"What?" Mitchell reaches for my hand, which is still sweeping rocks aside.

"Look, I don't know how I know, and I know it sounds completely crazy, but she's there." My eyes plead with him to understand.

"Okay. I believe you." He lets go and helps me clear the slab. Once we do, I can see that it's a three by three foot piece of concrete, but it's not normal concrete. It's a slab on top of a metal drainage system. "My God," Mitchell says.

"With all the rain we've been getting, she could be drowning down there."

"Help me lift it," I tell him. We each grab an end, and Dad and another officer help. We pull it up on one side, resting it against the electrical building. Ed couldn't come out now if he wanted to.

"Veronica?" Mitchell calls into the dark opening.

"I'm going down," I say, shedding my jacket in order to fit in the space, which is a round hole, much smaller than the concrete slab.

"No way. We have no way of knowing what's down there." Mitchell shrugs off his own jacket. "I'll go. Ed hasn't answered us, so it could mean he's down there, too."

I shake my head. "No. He's the one who covered the slab after he stashed her here. The only place for him to hide is in there." I point to the concrete building.

Mitchell nods. "Here." He takes a flashlight from his belt. "I'll hold this so you know what you're climbing down into. I'll toss it to you once you're down there."

I pat my phone in my jeans pocket. "Or I can use this."

"I'll light your way then." His eyes linger on me as I start to climb down the hole.

There are tree roots in the ground, but not enough to make climbing down easy. This was meant for rainwater, not people.

"Veronica?" I call. "Can you hear me? My name is Piper Ashwell, and I'm here to rescue you." My hands slip, and I fall to the ground, landing on something soft. "Veronica?" I take my phone from my pocket and turn on the flashlight. Veronica's bloody face comes into view. I immediately reach for her neck to feel for a pulse. I find one, but it's weak. Has she even had food or water in the past few days?

"She's here, but I'm going to need help getting her out. She's unconscious," I yell up to Mitchell.

"Hang tight," he calls back down, and it feels like ages before he lowers a rope into the hole.

"What did you do, make the rope yourself?" I ask as I tie it around Veronica's waist.

"You know me. I'm crafty like that."

I give a tug on the rope. "Pull her up." I guide her body, making sure she doesn't hit her head and do any further damage. The poor girl has been through the ringer already.

Once she's out, Mitchell lowers the rope down for me. "Your turn."

I tie it around my waist and extend my hands for the roots I used on my way down. "Nice and easy. I'm going to try to climb out once I can reach the roots."

"You got it, boss."

I smile at the nickname. "I could get used to that." Now that Veronica is safe, I allow myself to breathe easier. I don't give a damn if that concrete building becomes Ed's final resting place. We got to Veronica before it was too late. We won this one.

Mitchell lowers his hand to me when I come into view, which I appreciate since the rope was giving me rope burns. He pulls me out, and I see Ed Haynes being cuffed.

Dad meets my gaze. "Sorry, pumpkin, but you missed the action while you were busy playing in that hole."

"You know Piper," Mitchell says. "She can't resist climbing down a muddy hole and getting dirty."

"Admit it. You were relieved I volunteered to go," I challenge him.

He unties the rope from my waist. "Actually, your skinny behind was the only one that would fit down there."

I want to protest, but he's right. No man would fit down

that hole. Only two skinny women like Veronica and me. I turn my attention back to Dad. "So, how did you get him out?"

Dad shoves his hands in his pockets, and I can see he's trying his best to suppress a smirk. "See that opening in the roof? I shoved a flare down there. Smoked him right out."

"It was genius," Mitchell says with admiration in his voice.

The rain must have put out the flare—or one of the officer's did because it's no longer lit. I'm a little sorry I missed it, but I've had plenty of opportunities to see my dad in action. He's probably the greatest detective the world has ever seen. Definitely the best Weltunkin has ever seen.

I wrap my arm around his waist. "Let's go home. I need some sleep."

He sniffs my head. "And a shower, pumpkin. You are in desperate need of a shower."

CHAPTER TWENTY-ONE

Mitchell and I show up at the hospital at noon on Saturday for visiting hours. Veronica Castell had a severe concussion, a fractured skull, and was under the influence of a drug the medical staff had never seen before. Luckily, it was similar to the date rape drug, and they were able to flush it out of Veronica's system.

The nurses direct us to ICU where Veronica is being kept while she recovers from her ordeal. I don't expect her to be awake when we arrive, and the nurse gives us each a stern glare as she says, "This visit needs to be very brief. The only reason we are allowing it is because the doctor feels having the people who saved her stop by would be good for her recovery."

She means her mental recovery. Everyone in Veronica's life has betrayed her. Her mother for giving her up and accepting money as a substitute. Her father for caring more about his reputation than his daughter's wellbeing. Her stepmother—for lack of a better word for Darla—for plotting the kidnapping in the first place. Ed Haynes for actually kidnapping her and causing most of her injuries. And, of course, Will Catton for trying to kidnap her and also attempting to prostitute her out to his frat buddies. Unfortunately for Veronica, Mitchell and I are the best she's got.

Mitchell assures the nurse we're well aware of the severity of Veronica's condition and that we only want to bring her the flowers he's holding and wish her good luck. Naturally, Nurse Bossypants is taken by his smile and allows us in the room.

"Still flirting with everyone. You can't help yourself, can you?" I ask, stepping around the hospital bed to the small table. I reach for the bouquet of flowers and place it on the table so Veronica will see them when she wakes up. I make sure the attached card is in view as well.

"Jealous I'm not flirting with you?" he asks.

"More like relieved."

Veronica moans, and the machine next to her starts beeping. The nurse rushes in, flashing us a "What did you do?" look. I shrug, and Mitchell says, "I think she's waking up," in that innocent little boy voice he's perfected.

Veronica's eyelids flutter, and she falls back into a restful sleep. The nurse continues to monitor the screen.

"What's going to happen to her?" I ask.

The nurse eyes me and then walks to the door. At first, I think she's going to leave without answering me, but instead she closes the door over without clicking it shut. "Her father was here last night when she was brought in. He called a woman."

Becky? It would make sense to tell Veronica's mother she was okay.

"It was his sister." She nods to Veronica. "Her aunt. Apparently, she lives in Philadelphia."

"Near where Veronica goes to school," I say.

The nurse nods. "I guess they're pretty close. She's going to let Veronica live with her so she doesn't have to stay on campus." She doesn't say "or live with her father anymore," but Mitchell and I both know what she means. His picture has been all over the media, along with news of his multiple affairs. He'll be busy trying to salvage his reputation, and that will leave no time to take care of Veronica.

"Is she going to be okay?" I ask the nurse. My hand finds Veronica's, and I can't resist.

"Aunt Tara, what made you want to become a nurse?" Veronica asks, sipping her coffee in the quaint little café outside of campus.

"I just like helping people, I guess. Why do you ask?"

"I haven't decided on a major yet." Veronica shrugs one shoulder. "Daddy paid for me to come here, and I feel like I should do something with my life. I don't want to live in his shadow forever."

Aunt Tara leans forward and places her hand on Veronica's. "Well, we're always looking for volunteers at the hospital. If you want to stop by and check it out, I'd be happy to put your name on the list."

"Really? Do you think I'd make a good nurse?"

"The question is do you think you would?"

"I don't know. Maybe. I do know you do more good than Daddy's money ever will."

"Piper?" Mitchell places his hand on my arm.

When I open my eyes, the nurse is gone. "Her aunt is a nurse. I think that means Veronica will be okay."

Mitchell smiles. "Good. Now how about we go check in with your dad? He said to meet him at your office."

"He's calling a meeting at my office instead of the

station? That can't be good." He usually reserves that for reaming me out for not following police protocol, which I neglected to do multiple times on the Castell case. "I guess we better not keep him waiting then."

———

When we pull up to my office, Dad is standing in the doorway of Marcia's Nook, chatting with Marcia. As soon as he sees us, he says goodbye to her and starts our way.

I give Marcia a wave before unlocking my office and letting Dad and Mitchell inside. I toss my purse into the bottom drawer of my desk. "Okay, Dad, what did I do wrong this time?"

"Are debriefings like this typical?" Mitchell asks. "Just for future reference."

"There's something I need to talk to you both about." Dad motions for us to sit.

Mitchell narrows his eyes at me, clearly thinking I have some clue what this is about. I do have a hunch, but Dad's being careful not to touch me, taking a seat on the opposite side of my desk and leaning back in his chair, so I can't be certain I'm right.

Dad fixes his navy blue striped tie even though it's perfectly straight already. "To be honest, I wasn't sure how you two would get along together. You're both... How do I put this delicately?"

"Total pains in your ass?" Mitchell asks with a smirk.

Dad chuckles. "Well, one of you is, but I'm not telling which one."

Mitchell and I point to each other at the same time, making Dad laugh again.

"The point is," Dad says, "you surprised me. You got

over whatever it was you didn't like about each other, and you became partners."

Mitchell and I misjudged each other at first. I thought his constant flirting with anything in a skirt meant he was a womanizer. I was wrong. He's a sensitive guy who missed growing up with his mother to teach him about women. And he thought I was... Well, I'm not sure exactly. Maybe he didn't trust that my visions were real and needed to see for himself. Whatever it was, it doesn't matter anymore.

"We're all a team, Dad," I say, reaching across the desk for his hand.

He's too smart, though. He shakes his finger in the air in front of him. "Not going to happen, pumpkin. Your old man knows you too well."

"Okay, then hurry up and tell us what this is about. You're kind of freaking me out. I'm used to you just coming out and saying what's on your mind. You're beating around the bush. It's unnerving."

Dad sighs and places his hands in his lap. "Your mother thinks it's time for me to retire. She's been asking me to for years, but this time I think she's right." The sorrow in his eyes tells a different story.

"Are you sure this is really what you want?" I ask, not completely blindsided by the news like Mitchell, judging by the way his jaw has dropped. I'm sure he didn't anticipate losing his partner so soon. They've only officially worked one case together.

Dad spins the wedding band on his ring finger. "I don't think I'll ever truly be ready to hang up my badge, but I'm tired. Look how many cases I've brought you in on over the past few years."

The numbers have been increasing drastically, but I always suspected he was doing it for my benefit, helping me build my career. Dad's done things like that since I was a kid.

"And this case..." He huffs. "Walking in the rain for hours on end, my feet are killing me, and I soaked them in Epsom salt for two hours last night when I got home."

How long the case took is more my fault than his. The police were looking in the wrong direction while Mitchell and I questioned Darla Castell. They went east, while Ed took Veronica into the west woods. So many of my visions had water in them. I'm sure Dad thought that meant they should look in the woods that eventually lead to the Delaware River.

"The point is, I think you two would make great partners."

"I'm not a cop, Dad. I'm a PI."

Mitchell leans forward in his chair, his arms resting uncomfortably on his knees. He looks like he's about to address a child, not the man who taught him everything he knows. "Tom, is this why you finally agreed to take me on as your partner? You wanted to see if I could play nice with Piper?"

"I'm her father. I couldn't leave her stranded without a good detective on her side. Not everyone at the station believes in Piper's abilities. You know that as well as I do." Dad turns to me. "But we both know Piper is the real deal."

If only I was better at interpreting my visions. The information I need is always there. Piecing it together can be like erecting an exact replica of the Eiffel Tower out of Mega Blocks.

"Why not just cut back to part-time? Or you could come work with me." I perk up at that idea. "My office is plenty big enough for another desk. You could decide which cases you want to help out on and take vacation time whenever you want."

Dad leans forward and places his hand on my desk. He doesn't say anything, but I know what he wants me to do. Read him. But he's my father. I shouldn't need a vision to make me understand this is what he wants.

I shake my head. "I get it. But if you ever get the itch to help out with a case, my offer stands."

He smiles. "I appreciate that, pumpkin." He stands up. "Now I'm off to tell the higher-ups. Wish me luck."

I give him a hug, and Mitchell shakes his hand before he walks out of my office. I watch him get in his car and drive away. "I saw this coming, but it's still weird to think I won't be working cases with him anymore."

"Don't fret. You still have me."

"Such a comforting thought," I say, slumping back in my chair.

"Want to grab a coffee?" Mitchell motions over his shoulder to Marcia's Nook.

"Yeah, I could go for a coffee." I stand up and open my desk to retrieve my purse.

"On me. Leave your purse."

I close the drawer. "I won't say no to that."

Mitchell steps outside and waits for me to lock the office door behind us. "So, does this mean I get to call you 'pumpkin' from now on?" He cocks an eyebrow at me.

Mitchell's a great detective, but he'll never replace my dad. No one could. "I'll give you one guess what will happen if you do, and I don't need a vision to foresee this one."

He laughs. "No, I don't think I need one either."

Not right now at least. Not until we get our next case.

———

If you enjoyed the book, please consider leaving a review.

And look for *Read Between the Crimes*, coming soon! You can stay up-to-date on all of Kelly Hashway's new releases by signing up for her newsletter: http://bit.ly/2pvYT07

ALSO BY USA TODAY BESTSELLING AUTHOR KELLY HASHWAY

Lies We Tell (Lies We Tell #1)

Secrets We Keep (Lies We Tell #2)

Games We Play (Lies We Tell #3)

Unseen Evil

Evil Unleashed

Replica

Fading Into the Shadows

Into the Fire (Into the Fire #1)

Out of the Ashes (Into the Fire #2)

Up In Flames (Into the Fire #3)

Writing as *USA Today* Bestselling Author Ashelyn Drake

It Was Always You (Love Chronicles #1)

I Belong With You (Love Chronicles #2)

Since I Found You (Love Chronicles #3)

Reignited

After Loving You (New Adult romance)

Campus Crush (New Adult romance)

Perfect For You (Young Adult contemporary romance)

Our Little Secret (Young Adult contemporary romance)

ACKNOWLEDGMENTS

Huge thank you to my editor extraordinaire, Patricia Bradley. Your knowledge of mystery and grammar were equally helpful with this book!

Thank you to my social media manager, Amber Noffke, for keeping me on track and making sure word is spreading about my books. Also, thank you to my amazing VIP reader group, Kelly's Coven. You guys are the best.

I have to thank my family and friends for their continued support. And finally, thank you to all the readers. I hope you enjoy Piper's story.

ABOUT THE AUTHOR

Kelly Hashway fully admits to being one of the most accident-prone people on the planet, but that didn't stop her from jumping out of an airplane at ten thousand feet one Halloween. Maybe it was growing up reading R.L. Stine's Fear Street books that instilled a love of all things scary and a desire to live in a world filled with supernatural creatures, but she spends her days writing speculative fiction and is a *USA Today* bestselling author. Kelly is also *USA Today* bestselling romance author Ashelyn Drake. When she's not writing, Kelly works as an editor and also as Mom, which she believes is a job title that deserves to be capitalized.

 facebook.com/kellyhashway

 twitter.com/kellyhashway

 instagram.com/khashway

 bookbub.com/authors/kelly-hashway

CPSIA information can be obtained
at www.ICGtesting.com
Printed in the USA
LVHW110300070420
652470LV00002B/593